THE BETTER PART OF VALOR

SHAPE UP OR SHIFT OUT BOOK 4

MANDY ROSKO

CHAPTER

ONE

THE BILL IN HER HAND MADE HER STOMACH ROLL, AND RUBY placed a hand on the desk to steady herself. It would be worth it. This all *had* to be worth it, as it was her only option.

Losing family had been the absolute worst thing to ever happen to her.

One at a time, for varying reasons, they were just gone.

Her parents had left a hole in her and in her brother's hearts at a young age. Then, three years ago, her brother, Ryan, did the same.

Forty-seven was too young to go, and part of her hated him, maybe even blamed him for not trying hard enough to stay.

Not that he would have been the first man of his age to have a heart attack, but if he didn't give up, if he didn't let the years weigh on him so much... maybe he would have taken better care of himself.

Maybe he would have thought it was worth it to keep going, to keep living for Ruby's sake.

It was too much to had hoped he'd live long enough to finally find his missing daughters. That search had been part of what had taxed him.

Perhaps that's why Ruby picked up where he left off, since he couldn't anymore. It was her brother's unfinished business and her *last* hope of a familial connection with someone, anyone else. Those girls were out there.

Somewhere.

She had family out there somewhere, and she wanted to look for them, even if the bill in her hand was something that made sweat form on the back of her neck.

Ruby swallowed hard, her heart pounding as she thought of her shrinking savings.

"Uh, would you take some monthly payments?"

Paul Lapin, the private detective she'd hired, smiled softly at her from across the table where they'd agreed to meet for coffee. It made the crinkles on the sides of his dark eyes more prominent and made Ruby's stomach do a little flip.

Usually, Ruby's raccoon shifter prey senses spiked from potential danger when around predator shifters like Paul, who was a coyote. That didn't happen with Paul, though. The PI was oddly gentle. Add in that, plus his rugged good looks—he was over six feet tall with dark blond hair and kind brown eyes—and it took all Ruby had to not fall for her knight in shining armor.

"Yeah, I can make that work."

Ruby nodded, embarrassed, and looked back down at the number.

She'd received several quotes from other private detectives, and they were all less than what Paul was charging her, even though Paul had already cut his regular wage in half for her.

But she needed a shifter to do this job, and they were hard to come by. She couldn't have a human PI look into the situation because they wouldn't understand the dynamics. The many variables would confuse someone who didn't understand shifter dynamics, and if the PI didn't get the whole picture, they wouldn't be able to do the job.

How could she tell a human PI that her dead brother had been a raccoon shifter who'd fallen in love with a red panda shifter, and that the red panda's snobby family hadn't liked that their little princess had slept with a dirty raccoon?

No way that would work, especially considering that the conceited family still—after all these years!—refused to give any answers to what happened to Ryan's triplet daughters.

Ruby found that out the hard way. After Ryan died, she tried contacting them herself, hoping for some mercy after all these years, just to be ignored at every turn about where the triplets could be.

So, yeah, she needed a shifter to do this job.

And they were extremely difficult to come by.

"I will pay it," Ruby said, determined to find the money. She was embarrassed that he was doing so much for her for so little, and the deal he offered was so good that Ruby couldn't say no to it.

"I know, and don't worry, things are tough for many people right now."

"Right. Thanks." Ruby reached for her paper cup of tea—which he'd also paid for.

Jesus.

"The good news is that the family has responded."

"Really?" Ruby perked right up. "I thought they'd never... what did they say?"

"Threatened me with a lawsuit if I didn't back off," Paul said, reaching for his coffee.

"How is that good news?" Ruby's eyes bulged. She couldn't afford to be tangled in a lawsuit!

"Don't worry, I look at it as a first step. No one actually wants to be embroiled in a lawsuit—that shines a spotlight on the very thing they want me to stop digging into. When they see I have no intention of backing down, I expect someone will offer a morsel of information to make me go away."

"Really?"

"You'd be surprised how much of my job is waiting for people to crack and fess up." Paul nodded. "Someone will talk when they realize I'm close to tracking down the midwife they used."

This was good. So good that Ruby was suddenly more all right with the bill sitting on the table between them.

And she wished she could pay him more.

Ever since she found Paul, Ruby learned so much

about how his sort of business worked. He was incredibly open with her about what he did every day. He didn't dance around any details or hide anything.

If something was tedious, he told her.

If it required more work, she believed him.

"Thank you so much. I mean it," she said. "I just wish... is there anything I could ever do for you? Maybe if you ever have an event or something, I'll give you a deal on the food."

Paul laughed. "The lunches you're making me are already perfect, trust me. I feel like I'm robbing you every time you bring me stuff to eat. You bring me much more than one could eat alone"—he nudged the decorative paper bag at his feet—"and my assistant loves you for it, just so you know. He's in love with your banana loaves."

Ruby breathed a little easier.

She couldn't always pay Paul in actual money, so, in her more guilty moments, she got into her shop and prepared extra breads, loaves, small cakes, and sandwiches. Usually with ingredients that were about to turn, since buying them was also getting more expensive with the price hikes lately, but it was something.

"And do you like them? I mean, I know you'd rather have real money..."

"Your turkey sandwiches and lemon loaves are my new favorite lunch, trust me." He brought his coffee to his lips before putting it back on the glass table and suddenly fixing her with a serious gaze. "I know this has nothing to do with the business you and I are doing, but I told my family about your shop, so don't be shocked if you get a bunch of new customers over the next couple of days."

"I'll give them a nice discount for everything you're doing for me."

"No, you won't, and they shouldn't take it. You run a business, and you need to keep the lights on. If you've got coupons in the paper, that's all they'll be using. My gift to you, for the free lunches."

It wasn't a guarantee for anything, but having more customers coming in, especially in this economy when she was desperate to catch up on her bills and pay Paul what he was really owed, made the rest of the day seem a little brighter.

"Thank you so much, again."

"Don't mention it."

Paul opened the folder he'd brought with them, using a red pen to point out what he'd been doing over the last week, the calls he'd made, places he'd driven to, giving her a full breakdown of everything he did, so she knew her money wasn't being wasted.

There was a lot of driving around, interviewing, and people-watching in his line of work.

Also, a lot more Googling than she thought there would be.

"I've got it narrowed down to a few people who helped with the birthing, a couple of midwives who've since retired. I'll be checking in with them and seeing what they know about where the children went. I did a search for any triplets born this year as well. Not just girls, in case that turned out to be false."

Ruby nodded, looking over the paperwork and feeling her eyes start to cross with all that information.

"Most shifter children are homeschooled or attend schools in their shifter communities. In any case, I couldn't find any raccoons or red pandas enrolled together in the community schools or the public school systems in any of the districts in any of these states. I'm not done going through every state, though."

He'd gone through five states. Considering how many schools had to be in each state, that was a fucking lot already.

Jesus, that looked like so much work. It made Ruby's head spin. She no longer felt good about the baked goods she was paying him with.

"Don't worry, I'll find something eventually," Paul said.

"Are you sure?"

"Yes, it might take a while, and I'll work with you on the payment thing, but I'm here to help."

Not for the first time, Ruby's breath caught, a swirl of emotions hitting her and hitting hard.

Namely, gratitude and also curiosity. Why would he bother with a tough case like this from a woman who could barely afford to pay him what he clearly deserved?

She didn't ask. Part of her suspected why but was too terrified of being wrong to actually indulge the thought.

Besides, women her age—a respectable forty-six—didn't command attention like that from mysterious PIs the likes of Paul. Plus, she didn't know anything about him. Sure, he wasn't marked as mated, but that didn't mean he wasn't seeing someone. It was much more likely that he was just one of those kinds of men who had a hero complex—who wanted to save the princess and slay the dragons just for the fun of it.

She certainly wouldn't question it out loud. Asking if he was flirting with her while he was supposed to be doing a serious job was likely the best way for him to walk away from her and her case entirely.

"Thank you again, so much," she said. "I really... I don't know how to thank you enough for everything you're doing."

"Keep making me some of those lemon loaves, and we might call it even."

Ruby smiled, ducking her head and feeling much younger than she was. She reminded herself that middle-aged wasn't old, so she might as well bask in what little attention she got.

They spoke some more. Paul gave her the rundown of his plans for the rest of the week and assured her that whenever she could make a payment was acceptable.

Thankfully, Ruby's bakery was only a few doors down the way from the cafe she and Paul had their meeting at. Which was good because it meant she could walk back with all of the papers containing Pauls's updates.

The less gas she used, the better, especially with the prices of everything these days.

She unlocked the door and pulled off the sign that said she would be returning in twenty minutes.

Sadly, no one had been lining up waiting for her, but

that was to be expected. Paul had quickly learned her hours and knew to not call on her in the middle of a lunch rush. They only met during her slow times.

However, it was going on two-thirty, and it was time to prep the bread for those who came in for it for their dinners or desserts.

Ruby set the papers aside in the back room, determined to look over them later.

All of this effort had to be for something. Because the thought that she was putting so much time, effort, and money into this search just for the children to want nothing to do with Ruby and her side of the family?

Well, what could she do? She had to focus on the fact that at least she would have tried.

That's what she said to herself as she answered some emails and put some cheese rolls in the oven for a custom order.

I'm at least doing right by you, Ryan, she thought to herself.

But was she hoping for him to be able to rest in peace when the answer finally came?

Or was she hoping that for herself?

TWO

"How did the meeting with dreamboat go?"

Ruby rolled her eyes. Her morning staff member, Stephanie, was taller than Ruby and thinner, with golden-brown hair in a pixie cut. In contrast, Ruby had shoulder-length black waves that had more than a few grays mixed in. Stephanie was twenty-five and still in those exciting years that included an active social life and dating scene. Still, despite their differences, Ruby considered Stephanie one of her closest friends.

"Paul gave me the paperwork to show he wasn't wasting my time and told me my late payments were still acceptable."

"Uh-huh," Stephanie finished arranging the cupcakes in the display case and then leaned on the counter while Ruby counted the cash register. "But how was he? Did he ask you out?"

Ruby rolled her eyes again, though she couldn't help but be amused. She enjoyed her morning chats with

Stephanie, even when they included the good-natured teasing.

"*That's* never going to happen."

"Why not? You're a hot little thing, and he's definitely single."

Ruby frowned, looking at Stephanie. "How do you know that?"

"You can tell by looking at him."

"How?"

"What do you mean, *how*? Does he ever smell like perfume to you?"

"Well, no, but that doesn't mean—"

"And I've never seen a ring on his finger."

"But—"

"Most importantly, he's not marked. He's not mated. And a man his age would be, if he'd ever found his mate."

"It doesn't matter," Ruby said quickly.

"But it does," Stephanie objected. "You admitted that you felt something the first time you met him."

"I—I think I was just stirred up over meeting a..."

"A sexy guy?" Stephanie prompted. "You can say it."

Ruby sighed. It had been a long time since she'd been with a man, and she hated that her first meeting with Paul had jolted her feelings so much. "I hired him to do a job, and that's what's important. Eye on the prize, and that prize is finding my nieces."

"Not bagging the hot PI?"

Ruby shot Stephanie a look and closed up the till. "He's always been nothing more than professional. Which is precisely what I want, especially when it comes to finding my nieces. If he did ever make a move on me, I'd have to wonder what was wrong with him."

"Ruby, come on." Stephanie suddenly looked sad.

"Not because of me," Ruby covered. "Just that it would be... unprofessional."

"You're just too afraid to admit that you might have felt that fated mate pull."

She hadn't told Stephanie that. She'd not really even admitted it to herself—it was such a big idea she didn't dare! Not when it was much easier to conclude that her feelings toward Paul were just that of gratitude.

Especially considering his continued insistence that she take her time with the payments and just... everything... yeah, it was too easy for her mind to wander into places it really shouldn't.

Besides, she would never hit on him. That would be weird. Ruby wasn't even sure *how* to hit on someone.

Her last relationship had been long-term and had ended years ago. It was sad for her to admit, even to herself, that she had no idea what she was doing when it came to the dating game.

"It's entirely professional," Ruby reiterated as she went back to the ovens to pull out the next batch of pastries. "He's not looking at me like that."

"He's giving you these huge discounts!" Stephanie fell into step behind Ruby, pacing a new batch in. "And it's *not* just because he likes your baking. Come on, Ruby! That's super cute."

"He feels sorry for me, that's all, and that's perfectly

fine," Ruby said, returning to the counter when she heard the door chime.

"Good morning, Ruby!" One of her regulars, Sandy Mactire, entered, wearing a cozy sweater and silk scarf along with her trademark warm grin. Her blonde hair with white mixed in flowed around her shoulders, and not for the first time, Ruby wondered at how impossibly beautiful Sandy was for an older woman—Ruby could only dream of having the kind of style and charm Sandy had.

"Hi, Sandy!" Ruby greeted her, and Stephanie shouted the same from the back. "I have your dozen all ready for you."

"Lovely, thank you!"

Sandy was the matriarch of the local wolf pack and, in general, a friend to everyone in town. Ruby had never once felt frightened around the woman, even though she was a wolf shifter, one of the fiercest predators out there. Quite the opposite, in fact. Sandy and her husband Beau exuded the feeling of *protectors*, not predators, and Ruby had always felt safer when one of the two was around.

"I just beat the rush, it seems." Sandy gestured outside, and Ruby glanced out the front windows to see what she meant.

"Is there an event going on downtown?" she asked when she saw the crowd of people crossing the street and heading directly for the bakery.

"I don't think so," Sandy answered.

"Not that I know of," Stephanie added, straightening

her little apron and stepping behind the glass case with the muffins and cookies.

Ruby tried to frantically think if she'd posted a coupon recently and forgotten about it. Sometimes online promos filled up months in advance, so she had to get her applications in early, but she was usually pretty good at marking the calendar for those.

"I'll take a cup of coffee this morning, too." Sandy took her box of pastries and moved to the cash register for Stephanie to ring her up.

The bell rang as the door opened to the new customers. Ruby put on a bright smile and greeted them —all faces she didn't recognize but who all smelled like shifters.

Ruby relaxed a little when she picked up at least one rabbit. Prey animals were always more comfortable to deal with—which is why she'd hired Stephanie—a pika shifter—in the first place.

"Hello!" an older woman—not quite a senior, but not just middle-aged either, with a round face and hair done up in a messy bun—all but bounced over to the counter.

"Hello," Ruby said. "Welcome to Ruby Red's. What can I get for you?"

"We heard you make all kinds of amazing treats," the woman said, her eyes shining as she looked over the display cases. "Do you make cakes?"

"Absolutely, and we do custom orders as well."

"Nana Cheryl, they have carrot muffins!" A little girl who couldn't be more than nine years old pointed, getting her fingerprints all over the display.

"Yes, sweetheart, we'll be getting some of those. Roger, what are you getting?"

A tall man with dark blond hair and a short beard stepped up to the case to have a look. "Wouldn't mind some of those turkey sandwiches and the lemon loaf I've been hearing so much about."

Ruby blinked, puzzle pieces suddenly falling into place. "You're all related to Paul?" The words squeaked out of her mouth without her meaning it to happen.

"Yup, that's my boy." Roger grinned, shooting his arm out across the counter, hand waiting for Ruby to shake. "I'm Roger Lapin."

"Oh, right," Ruby said, taking his hand, too shocked to firmly shake back.

He didn't seem to mind and grinned beneath his beard. "You can call me Roger Rabbit if you want."

Ruby tilted her head.

Stephanie laughed.

"Please ignore my brother." Cheryl sighed and smacked his shoulder. "I promise, my nephew, Paul, is much better behaved than this idiot."

The little girl laughed, and Sandy—who'd taken her coffee and box of pastries to a table—did too.

"Sandy, I didn't see you there. Hello!" Cheryl gushed, and the two women talked for a moment while Ruby peered at the others waiting to be served. A few younger —teens to early twenties—stood behind Roger, and outside, several couples with children waited patiently.

"Paul said he had a big family," Ruby mused.

"Rabbits breed like rabbits, my dear," Roger said with

a shrug, looking over the breads and cheese rolls and sandwiches. "We don't just live off rabbit food, though. Can you pack up all those carrot muffins?"

The little girl gasped with glee, her eyes widening.

Ruby nodded, and Stephanie was already grabbing a box. There were only six in the display case, but this worked out well since she was getting worried some of them would need to be thrown away.

"Would you need more baked? I can get them ready for you if you need."

"Maybe just those for now," Cheryl said, returning to the counter from her chat with Sandy. "But I will also take your last two lemon loaves and those banana breads, if you will."

"Right, of course."

Ruby flew into action, her heart racing in a good way from this new rush of business.

Things had been slowing down thanks to the rising costs of gas and food prices, so having a dozen rabbit shifters in her small shop, clearing her out of most of her baked goods, felt amazing.

In the end, they took all of her carrot and apple cake muffins, a dozen cake pops for the kids, ten of her pre-made artisan sandwiches, six of her French bread loaves, four garlic loaves, and another ten of her cheese rolls.

There were a few other odds and ends in there, but even with the coupons added to the order, Ruby felt a tightening in her throat by the total bill, and then elation that the credit card swiped actually worked.

She and Stephanie packed up the whole order in multiple bags.

Some stayed and munched on the food, but Cheryl stayed the longest, sitting with Sandy. When everyone else had gone, and Ruby and Stephanie had made new batches of everything to toss in the ovens, Ruby returned to the table to check up on the women.

"Everything alright?" Ruby asked.

"More than alright!" Cheryl replied. "Paul was right. This was more than worth the trek here."

"Oh no, I hope you didn't come all the way out here just for baked goods!"

"Don't you worry," Sandy said. "They're doing some antiquing today, too. Isn't that right?"

"Sure is," Cheryl agreed. "Plus, I got to see my old pal, Sandy, here. It's been a truly fulfilling day, indeed!"

"I'm glad to hear it." Ruby smiled. "I'll have to thank Paul again for recommending the place to you all."

As if guessing what Ruby was thinking, Cheryle offered her reassurance that Paul didn't share any information of his client's cases. "He is incredibly professional like that, sweetheart, so don't you worry."

"I believe you."

"He only mentioned he liked your lunches and insisted we come along. We're going on a picnic, so this was perfect with your nice coupons."

Ruby nodded, still feeling choked up, still hardly able to believe Paul really did recommend her place and that his apparently huge family had actually come along.

"Paul has been very nice to me, and I'm so happy you came to try us out."

"Oh, we'll be back," Cheryl said, getting up to leave. "You just let us know if you need anything."

Really? "Right, I will, thank you."

"I should be going, too," Sandy said, standing with Cheryl. "The boys will be wondering where their breakfast snacks are."

"Thanks for coming in!" Ruby called after both women.

Finally alone again, Stephanie looked at Ruby with her mouth in an open smile, eyes glittering. "Seriously? Did that just happen?"

Ruby was too busy looking at the numbers on her terminal and blinking several times to make sure they were real to feel much of anything.

"I'm... I think I'm stunned."

"No kidding! I thought you said the private dick you were using was a coyote?"

"Oh!" Ruby snapped to attention, looking up and around as if she expected all those rabbit shifters to appear back in her shop magically. "I mean, he is. I'm sure of it."

"You scented it on him, or he told you?"

"I scented it on him, but I can't see how I'd be wrong."

"Maybe it's just that side of his family? That happens sometimes,"

Ruby cringed.

Stephanie knew Ruby was paying Paul to find her brother's children, but she didn't know the details.

Or how close to home her comment hit.

"Yeah, I guess you're right."

"Wait, what did you say that guy's name was again?"

"Paul Lapin."

"Oh, my God!"

"What?" Ruby asked, alarmed. "What?"

"Lapin is French!"

"Yes?"

"French for *rabbit*."

No way. "Are you serious?"

"Yes. I took French in school. Nothing much stuck, but I love bunnies. That word stayed with me." Stephanie laughed. "He's a coyote shifter from a family of rabbits."

"Coyote must be his mother's side," Ruby said, feeling dazed but finally understanding why Paul had such a gentle nature about him—he would have to, if he'd grown up surrounded by rabbits.

"He did say he had a big family."

"Rabbits usually are a big family," Stephanie said. "I'll get started on some more fresh rolls."

Ruby nodded, but her brain was still working.

Paul's mother hadn't come in with the rabbit family. What could that mean?

There were many different reasonable reasons. She could be stuck at work. She could be divorced from Roger. She could be deceased.

Or... did she give Paul up to the Lapin family and walk away because of pressure from her family? Had Roger gone through something similar to what Ryan had? If that *did* happen to Paul, it would explain why he was so... understanding about the situation with Ruby's nieces.

With one major difference: Paul at least had the rabbit side of his family. Ruby's nieces had been cut off from *all* family.

Ruby swallowed hard and followed Stephanie into the back room, determined to get to work and restock her shelves.

Regardless of Paul's reasons, she more and more owed him a debt now that he'd convinced his family to come in and nearly buy out the shop today.

At least, with his family's support, she had a chance of paying her debt back, leaving her more mental space to focus on what mattered the most.

Finding her nieces.

CHAPTER

THREE

Another month went by with little to go on.

Ruby expected that. All the research she did pointed to the fact that investigation wasn't like in the movies.

Information didn't come about within hours or days, and sometimes it could take years.

Paul was as generous as ever, only charging her for the bare minimum and still as gracious as could be whenever her payment was less than expected.

Of course, whenever that happened, someone from his family, either his father or his aunt, came into her bakery within a day or two with a giant order for more breads.

That wasn't the only time she saw them, though. With a family their size, there were two or three events every month this season, and since they all had differing tastes, every birthday or anniversary cake order was for at least four cakes.

Rabbits loved the spring, it seemed.

Ruby absolutely didn't care. She was quickly deciding that she adored Paul's rabbit family.

Every time she got an order from them, Paul got paid, and her credit card statements no longer looked so menacing.

Stephanie made more jokes about how Ruby needed to get off her ass and ask out Paul when this was over with, but Ruby ignored her.

"That's not what this is about."

"I know, but he keeps taking you for coffee,"

"They're meetings so he can update me on the progress he's making."

"Updates that could easily be done over the phone or Zoom? Sounds like he's asking you out for coffee dates in disguise."

Ruby rolled her eyes, figuring the best way to go about this was to let Stephanie's imagination wander and not say anything.

Paul was handsome, but Ruby wasn't about to let her mind wander. She had too much weighing on her heart without getting her hopes up about something else.

That evening, after Stephanie left for the day, Ruby was decorating an order of cupcakes for the Lapin family —with bunny heads and carrots made of icing, of course! —when the bell to the front door rang.

Ruby smiled and set down her piping bag, rinsing her hands before going to the front.

"You're a little early," she said, expecting it to be one of the Lapins, there for the cupcakes. "Oh, sorry, can I help you?"

The prim woman with the steely gaze staring back at her from the other side of the counter was *not* who she was expecting.

Nor was she any other familiar customer.

And Ruby couldn't identify what type of shifter she was.

The woman before her was slim, her hands holding a small clutch in front of her while she eyed the displays surrounding her. Her hair was straight, steel grey, and cut sharply at her jawline. Her clothes and heels gave off the impression she'd just come from tea and crumpets at a fancy clubhouse.

Her thin lips pursed when she finally looked back toward Ruby. "Your establishment appears decent."

"Oh, well, thank you." Ruby kept her smile glued in place, though she wasn't sure the woman was complimenting her. Maybe the dig was aimed more at the town than Ruby's shop, but either way, it didn't sit right with Ruby. "Would you like to place an order? We do custom cakes and tea biscuits."

Tea biscuits were a rare order, but she had to play to the customer.

"This will do." The woman seemed flustered and annoyed as she reached into one of the baskets along the wall, taking a single loaf of French bread.

Ruby nodded. "Absolutely, let me get a paper bag and ring it up for you."

She did everything she could to make the buying experience *decent* for... whoever this woman was.

The stranger had a familiar scent to her. She had to

be a shifter, but it was definitely an animal that Ruby didn't sniff around enough of.

Usually, the exotic animals threw her off. Their scents were always a little confusing at first.

But the lady on the other side of the counter kept staring at her as though Ruby had personally offended her somehow.

"Here is your order," Ruby handed the bag and the receipt over. "Thank you for stopping by, and I hope you will come by again."

Even though the woman was less than pleasant, Ruby reminded herself that she still needed as many paying customers as she could get, and she wasn't about to be rude and let someone spread that around town.

The woman took her bag, but she kept staring at Ruby with that frostiness in her slate-gray eyes.

Ruby couldn't take it anymore. "I'm sorry, is there something on me?" She glanced down at herself, not seeing anything on her apron other than some flour and maybe a little food coloring.

"I would like for you to call off your dog."

Ruby blinked at the woman. "Uh, sorry?"

Those steely eyes narrowed. "The coyote. Fire him."

Okay, Ruby dropped the whole *customer is always right* thing real quick, opting to stand her ground. "What's it to you what he does?"

"My family has been through enough. I keep getting calls that he has been... snooping."

Her family?

The woman's strange scent made a little more sense

now. Red panda wasn't something Ruby ever ran into—not since Ryan had dated one.

"That's his job, yes." Ruby's heart pounded. This was it. What she'd been waiting for. Now, she had to play her cards right, if she hoped to gain any information from this woman.

A woman she instantly hated, knowing she was part of the family that had been so horrible to Ryan.

A family that had gotten rid of Ruby's three baby nieces.

The woman took in a huff of breath. "You can afford to be selfish about this, but I cannot."

"*Selfish?*" Ruby's jaw dropped in shock.

"My daughter made the decision to give those children a better life. That is to be honored."

Oh, fuck this woman.

"A decision she made without my brother's say-so," Ruby snapped. "So, no. I'm not honoring your daughter *or* you."

"What was done was for the best," the woman said. "Even she came to see that in the end."

Ruby frowned. "In the end?"

The woman straightened up a little, her spine stiffening as she sucked in a breath.

Ruby understood right away. "Your daughter passed?"

A heavy hesitation. "Yes. Three years ago."

Three years. When Ryan died.

Ruby didn't want to think about what that could mean. It could be entirely coincidental.

Totally could mean nothing at all.

But there were cases of mates who, when one passed, the other wasn't so far behind.

Ruby didn't want to entertain the thought that Ryan had found his mate in some rich and stuffy red panda shifter, just for that love, and his whole life, to be ruined because of her family.

"My daughter found a nice husband later. She would never have been satisfied with a life with a... a *raccoon*."

Ruby glared at the woman in front of her. "No, she was just the sort of woman who let her parents manipulate her into giving up her babies and turning her back on her fated mate."

That seemed to be enough to make the woman in front of her look ready to go on the attack.

She might have done it, if it weren't for the counter between them.

"Do *not* speak of my daughter like that. She was a good girl."

"Not that good if she was rolling around with a gross raccoon."

Yeah, this lady definitely would have jumped the counter if given the chance. There was no doubt about that in Ruby's head by the nasty look she got for the comment.

"Call off your dog," the woman snarled. "I noticed that this strip is for sale. A new buyer could come in, raise the rent. You should take care."

Ruby opened her mouth, but there was no witty

comeback, nothing she could say that would turn the tides because, holy shit, could this woman really do that?

Ruby had no idea what the laws were on things like that, but as the woman walked out of her bakery—throwing the fresh French loaf into the nearest trash before disappearing—Ruby realized she would have to start learning.

CHAPTER

FOUR

The absolute worst part about any of this was feeling so helpless.

She had no idea what to do—for any of it! She didn't know how to search for people. She didn't know what calls to make, and there was only so much she could get online.

But that's why she was paying an expert. She had to remember that. She was paying Paul—well, paying whenever she could—to assist her in this matter, so she shouldn't feel so ashamed of *needing* the help.

Even if Stephanie wiggled her brows as Ruby went to coffee with him for another update.

Ruby could just roll her eyes.

But now that Paul was sitting in front of her, ignoring his paper cup while he went over the latest updates, she couldn't help but wonder if she should have told him right away about the red panda visit. Maybe even called him the night before, right after it had happened.

Why had she waited?

"I went through the schools in these other states, and more and more, I'm starting to believe the girls were separated. It makes sense. They'd be easier to track if they'd stayed together."

Ruby snapped out of her cloudy thoughts, her heart sinking. "Oh. That's... oh."

What was she supposed to say to that? Her heart absolutely sank.

Not only did her brother never get to meet his children, but they might not even know each other?

That was so damn horrible.

"I'll find them," Paul said. "Believe it or not, this is good."

"How is that good?" Ruby really didn't understand it.

"Because every bit of information I can get narrows it down. I was looking for three sisters housed together. Now I can search for young women, either raccoon shifters or red panda shifters, who were adopted out on their own. Then I can start narrowing it down by their birth years."

"R-right. Sorry. I should've... yeah, that makes sense." Ruby blinked, feeling a little stupid and a little bad for not entirely being on the same page. "So, how do you manage to look for people who were adopted out? I thought records like that were typically sealed up?"

"They typically are," Paul replied. "For humans. Luckily, being shifters, our laws are a little more... bendable."

Ruby nodded, the word *law* getting her brain

whirling as she remembered the threatening words of that mean red panda.

"There's something I have to tell you."

"Did something happen?" Paul had barely touched the lip of his cup to his mouth when she said it. He lowered it, giving her his full attention. By the time he managed to get any coffee inside him, it would be stone cold.

"Yeah," Ruby felt a rush of embarrassment as she explained what happened, even though she knew it was illogical.

It wasn't her fault one of the red pandas had come to see her. It wasn't her fault she was being threatened. None of this was her fault.

It wasn't her brother's fault either.

Even so, she still felt like a damsel in distress as she explained what had been said. She was just giving him one more thing to pity her for, right after *unable to pay full fees,* and *needs his family to come in and make giant purchases all the time.*

"I'm sorry," Paul said, not at all looking at her like she was pathetic. "I didn't think anyone from that family would try contacting you. Especially not Angela."

"Her name's Angela?" Ruby grimaced. "She was anything but angelic."

Paul laughed and shook his head. "You're not wrong about that. But yes, Angela is the biological grandmother to the girls we're looking for, and the matriarch of the family now. She's something else."

"That's saying something. Right down to her wasting a perfectly good loaf of bread," Ruby said.

Which had been, weirdly enough, more insulting than the disdain Angela had shown inside the shop.

Ruby wasn't sure if it was because she was a raccoon shifter or if there was something wrong with her head, but she despised food waste. Hated it so much that her inner trash panda fought with her to go out into the trash bin and rescue the loaf. *It was wrapped in a paper bag! Still perfectly good!*

She managed to stop herself.

It would be difficult to have a good reputation as a baker if the locals thought she was serving them garbage, after all.

Then Ruby realized something. "Has she been contacting you?"

"Not as directly as she reached out to you," he admitted, as calm and challenging to read as ever. "I have been getting voice mails."

"She told me to make you back off. I guess when you wouldn't..." Part of Ruby wanted to be angry, and she wasn't sure why. "Why didn't you tell me she was calling you? You said they threatened you with legal action but didn't say you'd heard from them directly."

"Because some details don't need to be disclosed if it's not beneficial to the client." He hesitated, his gaze stony. "But I'm sorry. I should have said something, as it might have better prepared you for what she was going to do."

Ruby nodded, appeased by his explanation. She

couldn't stay mad at Paul. He was doing too much for her, and who was she to question his professional decisions?

And she still needed his advice. "Angela threatened to buy the strip mall and increase my rent. Can she really do that?"

"Were you aware it was up for sale?"

"No," Ruby replied.

Paul seemed to genuinely think about it. "The owners should have notified their tenants if they were putting it on the market. Even if they expected a quick sale, they probably would have put up a for-sale sign—realtors love those if just to brag about the sale after the fact."

"Definitely no for-sale signs around," Ruby agreed.

"Then, there is the matter of Angela's assets and resources. The family has money, but I'm not sure even they would want to blow upwards of a million dollars or more to increase the rent for one tenant. I'd say she's just trying to scare you."

"Well, it worked," Ruby said, sliding her thumb back and forth across the lip of her paper cup. She snuck a glance at Paul, who was still looking at her with that unreadable expression.

The funny thing was? Being with Paul and having him there to offer her reassurances really made her feel better.

"Don't let them intimidate you," Paul said, and his hand moved toward hers.

Her heart raced illogically when he placed his hand

over hers. His hold was strong and warm, comforting too, and the following squeeze he gave had felt like it passed on an infusion of courage.

Then, just as quick as it had happened, Paul pulled his hand back, grabbing his cup of coffee.

"Well, thanks, anyway," Ruby said, desperate for her heart rate to slow. Why had such a small and quick touch excited her so? It was just a little gesture! "Hearing you say that... I know that family is well-off, but you're right. I mean, who buys a whole strip mall for something like that?"

"Not a very good business investment," he agreed, cracking a smile, so those adorable lines crinkled around his eyes again.

Right, now, she definitely felt better.

Ruby didn't like being so powerless, but as the situation went on, it was something she realized she was going to have to come to terms with. The shame of needing so much help, of having to take favors to get what she wanted done, was slowly simmering down to something she could manage.

Accepting help didn't always have to make her feel like she'd spent her night rolling around in a compost heap.

"Look, I know I said this all the time—"

Paul cut her off. "You're welcome."

Ruby sat a little straighter, then grinned at him. "Thought you were going to tell me not to thank you."

"I was thinking of that," Paul said, finally taking a sip of his coffee, then making a face at it as if it had personally offended him. He set the cup down. "But I know you would just ignore it anyway, so I might as well not fight it."

That made sense. "Your dad and your aunt are lovely people, by the way. I've been experimenting with so many different carrot recipes that most of my display cases are now filled with carrot cakes and carrot muffins. I'm even thinking of ordering carrot juices for the next time they come in."

Paul snorted softly, the soft crinkles that made him so handsome deepening at the corners of his eyes.

Ruby had to remind herself that this was a professional relationship.

"Sounds like them. Always with the salads and rabbit foods." He shuddered. "Family barbecues are a nightmare."

"What do they barbecue?"

"Unless I remember to bring steaks and burgers? Vegetable skewers."

He said it with such a twist of his mouth that Ruby laughed aloud. She couldn't help herself.

He looked beyond disgusted, and that made Ruby laugh harder.

It had been a while since she'd laughed like that. Since she had such a warm feeling in her belly.

Probably not since...

Ruby stood suddenly, clearing her throat. "Uh, I should get back."

Paul nodded and stood. "Of course, I didn't mean to keep you."

Part of her had hoped he would say something to get her to stay.

Oh, so soon? But you haven't finished your coffee yet. We should talk about your last payment. I might need to bump up my prices.

But no, nothing. He was as professional as ever, proving that this thing she was thinking about, but also not thinking about, was entirely in her head and not reciprocated in the least.

God, she had better things to be worried about than how pretty his eyes were.

"I'm going to head back. I already said that. Anyway, I just want to be there in case Angela decides to stop by again. I don't want Stephanie there by herself if that happens."

"I understand. I'll keep digging, but don't worry, I do think I'm getting close, and we will find them." He smiled that smile again that made the sunshine seem just a little brighter that day. "And my aunt loves your carrot cheesecake, by the way. If you keep making those, you'll have a customer for life."

"Right, well, she and pretty much every adult on that side of your family signed up for my newsletter. I'll have to send out some coupons for cheesecake."

She wouldn't mind it if he came by and tried some, too. He might be a coyote shifter, but even coyotes must love cheesecake, right?

On the way back to the shop, Ruby put Paul out of her mind and focused on the updates he gave her. Passing the open-stock refrigerator, she considered the pre-made sandwiches. She didn't sell a ton of them, but it might be worth adding an option of steak sandwiches and sending a coupon for that out.

That way, the Lapins could feed Paul some meat from time to time, whenever they had another one of their big bunny family bashes.

She still thought it was amusing that a coyote had a huge rabbit family.

She wondered if any of his cousins ever got nervous shifting into their animal shapes around him at family events, or if a prey animal could get used to the predator if they were around them enough.

"How was it?" Stephanie asked with a knowing little smile on her face.

Ruby ignored the implication, focusing on the information Paul had shared. "He's fairly sure the girls were separated. Which is sad for them, but he thinks this is still good news because it narrows down the sort of people he's looking for."

"Oh," Stephanie said, her expression suddenly becoming more somber. "Yeah, that's... yeah."

Ruby patted the girl's shoulder and went to the back room to check on her inventory.

It was a bit of a heavy subject, and she didn't expect Stephanie to take any of it well. The pika shifter was naturally empathetic, and while Ruby had kept her informed of most aspects of the case, it wasn't Stephanie's load to carry.

Still, even though Paul said it was good to have any information at all, Ruby couldn't help but be sad.

The girls didn't grow up together. They didn't get to be sisters.

They didn't get to braid each other's hair when they were getting along or pull it when they weren't. They didn't get to bully each other or defend each other from other bullies. They didn't get to do all of the sibling things that Ruby enjoyed with Ryan.

Ruby had no sisters, so she didn't know what that would have been like, but she couldn't imagine growing up without Ryan.

Ruby hated that her nieces didn't have that, though she could at least hope they hadn't felt lonely growing up. Maybe their lives had been good? Maybe they'd had other siblings in their adoptive family.

Ruby rubbed at her burning eyes, forcing herself to take a breath as she stared at her list of ingredients and supplies that needed to be restocked.

She heard the bell ring out front, deciding to let Stephanie deal with it.

About twenty seconds later, Stephanie appeared in the doorway.

"Uh, Ruby? Sorry to bother you. There's a lady out front who wants to see you."

Jesus. Angela again?

But maybe not.

"Not someone you know? Ruby asked. "Did she say her name?"

"No. I'm guessing it's your red panda friend."

Ruby looked back at her friend. "How do you know what that smells like?"

Stephanie shrugged. "A little of her nasty scent lingered the day after she came in. So, yeah, now I know what a red panda smells like."

Ruby sighed.

"Do you want me to tell her to get lost?"

Ruby loved this girl. She really did. "No. I'll do it."

The bravery that Paul had filled her with when he'd pointed out she likely couldn't really buy the strip mall and increase her rent was still there. Enough that Ruby wanted to deal with this on her own.

She quickly stepped up to the front, setting her face in a stern, *don't mess with me,* glare as she prepared herself for the second face-off.

Only to find that it *wasn't* Angela on the other side of the counter. Ruby almost stumbled over herself, taking in the sight of the younger woman—maybe still in her twenties—with wavy red hair and an adorable dusting of freckles on her cheeks.

So, Angela sent another family member to send a message, she thought, keeping the scowl on her face as she asked. "Can I help you?"

"Oh, hi." The young woman straightened her back, her eyes a touch wide as if she knew she shouldn't be there. "Uh, I'm just... looking?"

Ruby nodded, staring long and hard at the woman and waiting for the snide comment or accusations. The woman quickly looked away, unable to hold eye contact for long, and went to inspect the bread loaves in their baskets along the wall.

If this girl bought some just to throw them out, Ruby would have kittens.

The young lady gently took a French loaf, like her... mother? Grandmother?

Either way, she brought it to the counter before inspecting the pastries and muffins behind the display case.

"Lot of carrot options," she said.

Ruby felt her hackles rise up. Was that a dig at Paul's family?

Stephanie answered before Ruby could open her mouth and say something she'd regret. "The carrot muffins with the cream cheese frosting are amazing. I totally recommend those."

"Yeah?" The young woman brushed a bit of hair behind her ear. "Okay then. Can I get six of those?"

"Absolutely," Stephanie said, pulling out a box.

Ruby took a breath, forcing herself to calm down and follow Stephanie's lead. So far, the woman had shown none of Angela's foul attitude, and Ruby started to wonder, what if she wasn't associated with Angela at all?

It *might have been* just a coincidence. The woman could just be another red panda shifter—rare as they were, it wasn't unheard of—who had nothing to do with Angela.

Right.

With that in mind, Ruby put on a real, proper customer service smile as she rang up the order, even offering ten percent off. "First-time newsletter subscriber discount. And I regularly send out other offers in the emails, so they're not just useless junk clogging up your inbox."

"Oh, sure, that sounds nice." She filled out the form with her name and email address.

"Ray Donaldson," Ruby read. At least now Ruby could ask Paul about her and how she was related to Angela. "Here are a few extra rainbow cookies for you, as a thanks for stopping in." And because Ruby felt a bit bad for being so unpleasant at first.

Ray's face lit up in a genuine smile. "Thank you so much. That's... really nice."

"We hope you come back. We're open seven days a week."

Ray nodded, continuing to stand there. Her mouth opened and closed once or twice before she abruptly turned and walked out of the bakery with her goods.

Ruby watched her go, pleased to see that Ray didn't toss her baked goods into the nearest trash can before she hurried across the street.

A man was there, waiting for her with eyes so striking and blue Ruby could see them from across the street.

They quickly walked off together.

Her boyfriend, Ruby assessed after he put his arm around her waist.

"Who was that? Someone from Bitchface's family?" Stephanie asked.

"Wow." Ruby stared at her, shocked that Stephanie had said such a thing.

"What?"

"You were so nice to her." Ruby laughed a little. "If that's what you were thinking the whole time, you're a better actress than I thought."

"It's a gift," Stephanie said with a shrug. "So, who was that?"

"Don't know," Ruby said, looking down at the name and email provided. "You think you could watch the store for a little while so I can—"

"Yup, already on it. Go, go, hurry up before you lose them."

Not for the first time, Ruby thought about how much she loved Stephanie. "Remind me I owe you a pay raise."

"I remind you every month. I'll get it eventually."

"Right," Ruby said, rushing into the back, her cheeks a little warm as she was reminded that it wasn't just Paul she owed.

She quickly yanked herself out of her clothes and shifted. Her raccoon shape had a good coat of fur, but not overly puffy and obvious.

She could be quick, sneak around, and still follow the interesting red panda shifter and her boyfriend to see what they were up to.

She was tired of leaving all the leg work to Paul anyway.

CHAPTER
FIVE

It had been such a long time since Ruby had followed anyone. Let alone when she'd done it in her raccoon shape.

It was a strange feeling. Her heart raced as she struggled to keep up with the red panda girl and her boyfriend, who smelled a little like a bear and... something else.

Ruby couldn't place it, but the bear smell alone was enough to make her instinctively want to keep her distance.

Having so many coffees with Paul had almost made her forget her aversion to being near any strange predator shifters. She'd gotten used to the coyote scent, which no longer alarmed her.

A bear, on the other hand?

Yeah, she was definitely keeping her distance.

Which meant she did a lot of her following the hard way.

Being on the ground level would have been a mistake. Absolutely anyone would have noticed a raccoon chasing after a couple of people on a sidewalk.

For that reason, Ruby had to climb a couple of fences, get up a wall, and run along the edge of the roof of another strip mall.

The worst part was that she didn't even know if what she was doing had a point, other than she wanted to find out where this woman had come from, to prove to herself that she wasn't sent by Angela to spy.

Though why she cared which side the girl was on, Ruby couldn't figure out.

Ruby's heart sank when Ray and the bear-man crossed the street to go into the park.

But then, they stopped walking. They were a little ways away from the road, but Ruby could just make them out down the path as Ray opened the box of carrot muffins and began eating one while the bear pulled out his phone.

Ruby watched them talk. Were they giving updates to Angela? Or someone else in the family?

The bear shifter eventually hung up his phone, giving his full attention to Ray, but Ruby couldn't discern a thing they were saying. Not from so far away, even with light traffic and good weather.

She leaned forward, trying to see as much as she could, even though she wasn't good at lip-reading, and they were too far off for her to make out lips anyway.

It was then she almost slipped!

Fuck! Pay attention! She skittered back from the edge of the building, cursing herself for the carelessness.

Ruby made sure her footing was secure before peeking over the edge of the roof again.

That had been a little too close.

Ruby might be doing something reckless—and maybe a little stupid—but she wasn't as young and nimble as she used to be, and a fall like that would have definitely hurt.

Ray and her boyfriend were still talking. They either had a lot of time on their hands, or it was a heavy conversation. Either way, Ruby was convinced that Ray's visit to her bakery wasn't just a coincidence. She'd gone in for a reason, and she was now talking to the bear—and whoever had been on the phone—about it.

Which meant Ray knew something about what was going on with Angela.

Though... now it almost looked as though the bear shifter was consoling her. Ray leaned into his chest, holding what was left of the cupcake in her hand, while the bear shifter held her close.

Ruby needed to call Paul. She should have done that first. He was the expert on following people around and taking notes.

Honestly, what had she been thinking? Chasing after them like this?

She knew better. PIs followed people for hours upon hours, days at a time, before finding useful information.

If ever.

And she thought she could chase a couple down for fifteen minutes and get some kind of breakthrough?

She wasn't even sure if she knew what she was looking for, which was the worst part.

Damn.

Well, she still had Ray's name and an email address, which was something.

Ruby turned and raced back to her bakery before she could be seen by another person.

Or worse, another animal.

She'd actually followed Ray and her boyfriend for several blocks, which had been a bit of a shock. Ruby must have been really caught up in the moment because she'd barely noticed the distance at all when running after them.

She sure as hell noticed it on the way back. Her poor little paws were killing her, and she gasped for breath, struggling when she dragged herself back into her shop.

Stephanie was in the backroom drinking a coffee while Ruby gathered up her clothes and waddled into the bathroom to shift back into a human and dress.

Ruby was so glad her paws could hold onto things. She shivered to think of having to grab her clothes in her mouth the way a wolf of a coyote shifter needed to.

She snatched a flyer off the bulletin board and fanned herself with it when she re-entered the breakroom.

"What happened?" Stephanie asked, her eyes wide with worry.

"I learned I need to start using my gym membership, is what happened."

Stephanie snorted. "Okay, but beyond that?"

Ruby shook her head. "I don't know. I need to make a call."

"Yeah, sure." Stephanie blinked at her. "You want me to get the sourdough started?"

"Yes, please," Ruby said, realizing she had forgotten entirely. If it weren't for Stephanie, Ruby didn't know how she would have kept her head on straight with everything going on. "You're a saint."

"I know."

Ruby moved to her office, grabbed her phone out of her purse, then stopped, holding it in both of her hands, thinking about what she would say.

Actually, she found herself being nervous about dialing his number *at all*. She hadn't called him since she'd first reached out to PIs. Now, he usually called her, but they just texted or emailed for the most part.

What was she going to say to him if he answered?

Another red panda came in, and while she didn't make any threats, I decided to follow her and her boyfriend like a total creep.

She sighed, annoyed with herself, but she needed to say something, so she shot him a text.

Hey Paul, I just had another red panda in my shop.

She went to the front, where the newsletter signup sheet was, and she included the woman's information in her text to Paul.

Just wondered if you recognized the name. Seemed

strange that I'd get another red panda in here the day after Angela was here, but she didn't say she was there for Angela, so it was just weird. She left with a bear shifter man.

She left out the part where she'd followed the pair so far down the road and to the park.

Jesus, Ruby still couldn't believe she'd done that.

Paul replied right away.

I'll look into it.

There was nothing else to it. Nothing that suggested he suspected she had gone out and actually followed a couple of complete strangers. Why would there be? It's not like she had a history of stalking her customers!

The door chimed, and one of her regulars walked in. Ruby shoved away her phone and the newsletter list and greeted her customer. With how often she abandoned Stephanie to meet up with Paul and now, to chase after customers, Ruby decided she needed to put some focus into work.

Paul would find Ryan's daughters. She had to trust his process and stop putting too much pressure on him.

And to herself.

She got back to work.

PAUL COULD FIND NOTHING IN ANGELA'S FAMILY ABOUT A young woman named Ray.

His first instinct was that the young woman used a fake name and fake email, but a web search pulled up social media profiles for a Ray Donaldson connected to that email account.

Jackpot. The jobs of a private detective had become so much easier in the digital age, thanks to all the information absolutely everyone was willing to share about themselves online.

The profile was of a young woman with dark red hair. Besides that, there wasn't much to be gained from her other photos or posts since Ray didn't update much. She'd made the last post just over two weeks ago when she'd apparently been getting ready to go on a dating cruise.

Time to dig a little further. What had she been tagged in? Many posts from friends, but the ones that interested him? Two in particular: 'only child appreciation day' and 'adoption awareness day.'

His adrenaline spiked.

Ray appeared to be about the age he was searching for, and he thought he saw a little of Ruby in the shape of this young woman's nose.

That might just be his bias. He'd been meeting with Ruby in person a lot—more so than he would any other client—and he had to admit he had more than a professional hope that he'd be able to reunite Ruby with her nieces.

He tried to tell himself it was only because he was big on family—with so many rabbits in his bloodline, he had to be—and Ruby was searching for her family. She was trying to repair what her brother couldn't while he was alive, and her situation tugged at Paul's normally tough heartstrings.

However, he'd felt sorry for clients before and never gone to the lengths he had for Ruby. From the in-person meetings to the extra hours he was putting in, the significant discount on his services, and his willingness to take payments, often short of what had been agreed upon.

Not to mention his out-of-the-ordinary request for his family to stop by her bakery. Thank God everyone on the rabbit side of his family had a sweet tooth. They paid Ruby for their cakes, and she got to pay him for his time, so it all worked out well.

Why did he go to such lengths for Ruby?

He wasn't yet ready to acknowledge it. Not until the job was done. Only then could he turn his detective's eye onto his feelings toward her and maybe finally admit that Ruby meant something to him beyond that of a client or even just a friend.

He printed off a photo of Ray and added it to his "maybe" files. Ruby was convinced Ray was a red panda shifter from the smell, but she could be wrong. It wouldn't be the first time someone misidentified another shifter's scent.

He stared at the photo.

No. He trusted Ruby's judgment on this. She hadn't smelled many red pandas in her life, and after her run-in with Angela, she would have a good feel for what that scent was.

Time to move on to more direct investigation.

He had contacts at the local hotels, motels, and beds and breakfasts. He started with the most logical accommodations—the affordable but clean and safe motels—and hit paydirt with his second call.

"Wait, yeah, I was here yesterday. She didn't check in herself, but I saw a redhead."

"I'm texting you the photo," Paul said. "She look anything like this?"

He'd played with the idea that Ruby's nieces could also be searching for her. Wouldn't be the first time that happened. Maybe it was happening now?

"Yeah, yeah, that's her. She and a few other people checked into a couple of rooms."

"How many? Did she have a male with her?"

"Yeah, a tall guy who smelled like a bear. Then two other men and two other women."

"You got any smell on the others?"

"Guys had something weird about them, but I didn't get close enough. Just noticed it when they walked through the lobby. The women, I'm pretty sure I'd say raccoon."

Well, holy shit.

He asked how many days they had checked in for, thanked his contact, and hung up.

He had to make some plans.

It could be a coincidence. Despite popular opinion, those did happen from time to time.

But a red panda traveling with two raccoons? If his contact was right, this would be *too big* a coincidence.

He just had to figure out how he would approach them and make himself known without scaring the living hell out of them.

If it *wasn't* them, he had to figure it out before Ruby got her hopes up.

If it *was* them, then he needed to reach out and facilitate a meeting before Angela found out.

Rita gripped Dallas' hand when the door promptly slammed in her face.

She blinked, shocked, her brain struggling to keep up with what just happened.

"What the hell?" Dallas said, knocking hard on the door three times before Rita pulled him away.

"Don't, we shouldn't," she said.

"She just—"

"I know," Rita said, rubbing the back of her neck. "But we should leave it. They don't want us here."

"You barely said who you were."

"Yeah, and they don't want us here."

Rita had been expecting that kind of reception. She also expected to not feel much about it. And she didn't. She'd been ready for it.

But she was glad Ray and Roquette weren't there to see it.

"Let's just go," she said. "I mean, this might not even be the right house."

Dallas made a face like he definitely doubted it could be the wrong house.

"You said your name and barely got out that you were looking for your family, and she slammed the door in your face." His cyborg eyes glowed red. "Makes me wish I could still shift so I could—"

"Don't say that," Rita slapped his arm. "We're still on her front step. She might have one of those doorbell cameras that record video and sound."

Dallas glanced around, then nodded. "Yeah, I guess we should go."

Rita smiled, loving him so much when he kept holding her hand as they walked away from the house.

"Their lawn is way too perfect," Dallas eventually said, glancing back. "You don't want to be related to someone who trims the bushes that flat."

Rita laughed a little, then pushed herself up to her toes and kissed his cheek. "Thank you."

"For what?" He growled a little, his body tense. "I should kick the door in."

"No, let's just head back. You're right. It might not be the right house anyway, and even if it is…"

Dallas looked at her, waiting, but Rita couldn't get the rest out.

"Too perfect," she finally said, then pulled out her phone to find out where her sisters were. "Roquette is still checking out the town. Ray got us cupcakes."

"Babe?"

Rita looked up at Dallas. He no longer looked furious. He seemed worried.

"Are you sure you're okay?"

Rita looked back down at her phone, wondering what she was supposed to say when she saw her sisters again.

"I am. It's weird, but this doesn't bother me. If anything, I'm just glad to know where I stand with that family."

"But your mother—"

"Would have kept us if she wanted us. Yes, for whatever reason, Ray believed that our mother was forced to give us up, but it was just a childlike wish."

"That woman looked older than your mother." Dallas looked back toward the house as though he were considering going back.

Rita pulled him along, back to the rental car. "Besides, could you imagine if I had to grow up in that house? Probably the sort of place that dished out spankings like penny candy for getting dirty or running indoors."

"Just sounds like the kind of place you would have honed your burglary skills," he teased.

She chuckled. It was those very skills that had brought her to him.

"You sure you're alright?"

Rita sighed. "I just don't want it hurting Ray or Roquette."

Dallas let his thumb slide across her hand. It was such a gentle gesture, but it was enough to make her eyes burn.

"I swear it doesn't bother me," she said, scrubbing at her eyes before the burning could get any worse—or turn into tears. "It's not about that. Or that woman. I swear."

Dallas pulled her close, his arm coming around her shoulder, letting her lean on him. Rita had always loved and prided herself on her ability to control her emotions. To be strong when shit was hitting the fan.

That was part of how she'd come to meet Dallas. A good raccoon shifter thief couldn't break into other people's houses and steal their shit if they couldn't get a grip on her emotional state.

"Ray and Roquette will be fine," Dallas promised. "You will be fine. You three have each other now, and that's what's important."

He was right. Rita took a breath and desperately pulled some calm into herself.

She'd done worse. She'd faced situations that had left

her heart slamming and her palms sweaty. She'd pushed through adrenaline rushes the likes of which would put that old, prim, snotty bitch into a shivering shame in a corner somewhere.

"You're right," she said. "Yeah, you're right. Let's get out of here."

She gripped Dallas' hand tightly, smiling up at him while feeling so damn grateful to have him.

At least now she had some answers. The most important answers, if she were honest with herself.

She didn't know what happened to her mother or what the situation was with that side of the family. But, at least now she knew she and her sisters weren't wanted by the red panda side, and that was all she needed to let these people go.

CHAPTER
SEVEN

Roquette was so done with traveling.

Was it wrong to dream of staying in one place for a little while?

She tried to remind herself that this could be it. The last stop on the family reunion tour.

It was, after all, the last clue they had that could connect them with their family.

A year ago, she couldn't have imagined that she'd connect with two women and learn they were her long-lost *triplets!* Yet, here they were.

And Arron? Her cyborg boyfriend? She would have laughed if anyone had told her she'd be happily settled down!

But it was true. So far, everything was turning out well.

As well as it could be, all things considered.

"I don't like waiting," Roquette groaned.

"You can still head out." Aaron smiled at her, his

mechanical eye glowing softly compared to the organic one. "I'm good with sticking around here."

Rita went to see the red panda, and Ray was currently spying on the raccoon side of the family. Roquette, the little coward she was, volunteered to stay behind with Aaron, buying food and other supplies and "checking out" the town.

A stay they didn't know would be brief or not.

They got their groceries. Their luggage was put away, and Roquette kept checking her phone for more possible news.

"Rita's apparently coming back with carrot muffins."

A quick text from Rita filled her in on why she was glad she didn't bother going out.

The bitch slammed the door in my face. Coming back now.

Right. Roquette might have actually cried if she had been there and that happened.

Aaron sat on the bed next to her. "You okay?"

She nodded. "Yeah. I'm good."

Aaron put his mechanical arm around her shoulders. It felt cold physically, but her entire body warmed by the touch, and she leaned into him, needing more of it.

"I'm just tired," she said. "Thank you for coming here and doing this with me. Us."

Aaron kissed her temple. "You're welcome."

She loved that about him.

He didn't say things like, "There's nothing to thank me for." He didn't pretend that this whole thing wasn't some giant nuisance.

She knew that he longed for some settled time, just as she did. They had barely gotten a moment's peace since the Baer sisters conspired for them to meet at their Christmas party that past December.

That's because it was at the party when Harmony Baer revealed her big surprise: she'd found Roquette's sister, Rita

Roquette had known there was someone else out there. They were separated at birth. She just hadn't known there was a third.

Not until all three of them ended up on Esme's matchmaking cruise.

The vacation had been both a romantic getaway for her and Aaron, as well as a family reunion of sorts. A time for her and Rita to get to know each other.

That had been going well, and then they'd found Ray. Their third sister. A red panda, whereas the other two were raccoon shifters—Roquette, a rare white one.

And then it was time to put together all the pieces. All three sisters had—to various extents and at different times in their lives—tried to track down their birth parents.

Ray had gotten further than either Rita or Roquette had. She'd known she had sisters, and she was also the one to find that they had an aunt.

"It feels like we haven't stopped since this entire thing started." She looked at Aaron, at his eye, his metal arm. If she put her hand on his knee, she would feel more implants from his prosthetic legs. "I feel so stupid, complaining like this."

"Don't feel stupid. It's a lot." Aaron seemed to think about something. "I can get my sunglasses back on, put on some gloves and a jacket if you want to head back out. Not too late to walk Ray and Bill back here."

"You don't have to cover up every time we go out." Roquette hated that for him.

He stroked her arm. "I don't mind. I kind of stick out a little, don't you think?"

"Not in a bad way," she insisted, needing him to know it. To believe it the way she did.

It was something they seemed to be constantly dealing with.

Her constant fears that she was being too much trouble, more than she was worth with everything going on with her family.

And Aaron's beliefs about himself and his looks.

He never outright said it, but it was in the little things. Always offering to cover his face or arm with sunglasses and long-sleeved shirts. He was clearly self-conscious about it. He just refused to talk about it.

Because of course he did. He had to feel like a tough guy.

With everything Roquette put him through, dragging him around the country, constantly moving and searching and traveling, she didn't want to pry too hard. Didn't want to force him to talk about something he clearly wanted to leave in his past.

But his eyes, even the glowing mechanical one, always seemed to soften just a little when she told him he didn't stick out like a sore thumb.

"You're a very kind liar, and I want cupcakes." He got to his feet. "Come on. We're going for a walk."

"I don't know,"

"We can't hide in here the whole time," he said, holding out his metal hand. "Come on." His tone was gentle, despite the words.

Roquette knew she could cross her arms and refuse to move or do anything at all, and he would still be his annoying, supportive self.

Might even leave their room to give her some privacy, using the carrot cupcakes as an excuse to spare her feelings.

She wanted to be stubborn but didn't at the same time. Since she didn't know what she wanted, she figured she might as well let Aaron take care of her.

She took his hand. "Maybe we could walk around a little."

"Right? We could walk into that bakery Ray just came from."

"You think they would notice I look like Ray?"

"Might be a fifty-fifty split," he answered. "Depending on how many customers your aunt gets, most people don't remember faces that well, and your blond hair is much different from Ray's red. Plus, you don't have the freckles."

"It would be funny to walk in and see if she notices something is up," Roquette said. "Wait for a reaction."

Aaron grinned at her. "You're loving this whole triplet thing a little too much."

She grinned back at him. "Maybe."

In truth, aside from the fact that she now had a whole family, three sisters and maybe an aunt and a mother and a grandmother, and other people in her extended family, the triplet thing excited her almost as much as all of it put together.

As a little girl, she'd always wished for siblings. A twin would have been fantastic, just for the fun they seemed to have on TV and in movies.

Finding out she was a triplet as an adult was beyond her wildest dreams.

"Let's go," she said, pulling Aaron to the door, suddenly feeling so much better.

They locked up behind them, deciding to leave their rental car and just walk. The town seemed nice and cute enough. Real middle-America sort of place, and Roquette was eager to see the shops and walk around.

The truck that pulled into the parking lot wouldn't have taken up much of her attention at all, but Aaron was on alert, snapping his head toward it before stopping and suddenly pulling back just as they were at the end of the parking lot.

"What—"

"Stay here," he said, his red, mechanical eye glowing beneath his sunglasses.

"Why?"

She looked past Aaron as he left her, heading back in the direction of their room.

The truck had parked in the nearest open spot, and a man with dark blonde hair had gotten out. Roquette crept closer, wanting to get a better look at the guy.

He didn't head to one of the other doors. He moved to her and Aaron's, and he didn't knock. Roquette realized he was scoping the place out.

She thought of Aaron's old boss, the vampire woman who was still messing with Dallas and Aaron. Had she found them? Was this guy working for Lilly?

Aaron and Dallas had said there were others—cyber-enhanced men that Lilly had once controlled. Even Bill had once worked for her.

The man at their door? He did appear to be on some kind of business, but he also looked older than most of the men in Lilly's circle—she usually went for men in their prime, who would be in the best shape to endure her cyber experiments.

Aaron did have a pistol on him, hidden beneath his shirt, and he also had a metal arm that could break bones if he put enough effort into it.

Which apparently wasn't much effort at all, according to him. Still, Roquette was nervous as he approached the man scoping out their door.

"Can I help you, buddy?" Aaron asked, stopping a few feet away. He always said the best defense was prevention.

The man turned, looked Aaron over, then noticed Roquette standing at the back of the parking lot.

Was he working for Lilly? She didn't see any cyber enhancements, but that didn't mean he didn't have any. She caught the slight scent of something canine-like. Not quite wolf... she couldn't put her finger on it.

Roquette took out her phone. She needed Rita and

Ray to get their asses back there and bring Dallas and Bill immediately.

"Yeah, I think I've got something for you," the man replied.

Roquette's heart hammered when the guy reached into his back pocket, her mind racing to the only thing he could possibly be going for as she ran over to help Aaron.

EIGHT

RUBY HAD A COUPLE OF LAST-MINUTE ORDERS THAT WERE called in, and even though she was tired, even though she was eager to get an update on that red panda who came in, she couldn't help but be glad.

Ryan used to tell her that the consistent blessings that came in life were always small and always there. Clean water, good food to eat, sunny skies, one of her delicious cakes.

And unexpected customers right when she needed them the most.

She could be tired. She could want all of this to be over, and she could be a little impatient, but Ruby was beginning to fall into the mindset that, even if the answers she looked for took longer to find than she'd hoped, things *were* going to work out.

She only wished Ryan was still around to enjoy it.

The carrot cake wouldn't need to be made up

tonight, so all she did was portion her dry ingredients, wrap them up, and put them away.

The sourdough breads needed more time, so she actually had to prepare the dough and wrap that up for the night before she could shut off the lights, turn on the alarm, and head home.

The twilight sky was pink and a little purple when she pulled up to her house.

Ryan's house.

The house she would gladly give back to him in a hot minute if he could come back.

He'd worked hard for it, but there was still a mortgage attached, and she was determined to pay it, to keep one of the few things of Ryan's that he'd worked hard for.

He never outright said it, but Ruby got the impression that he'd wanted a house—a home that he owned—with a bit of land so that, one day, if he did ever find his girls, he could show them that he'd made something of himself. That he was a raccoon shifter, but one that had built something.

Something he could pass onto them, should they ever want it.

Now Ruby lived there, but it wasn't her house. Not really. It would go to the girls, the young women, if they wanted it.

Ruby slid her key into the lock just as her phone buzzed.

She dropped down onto the deck, digging through her purse to pull the damn thing out before the ringing could stop.

Paul's name was on the screen. Ruby's heart slammed in her throat as she accepted the call and put the phone to her ear.

"Hey, did you hear anything? Find anything out? About the woman?" She couldn't seem to get one thing out at a time, but that was all right.

Much of her purse had been dumped out onto the deck, old receipts and tissues blowing away in the wind, but none of it mattered when she heard Paul's voice.

"I have something for you. Something major. Where are you now?"

She blinked. "What do you have? Another lead? Did that woman know something?"

"There is a lead, yes, but it points straight at that young woman."

Ruby froze. Her brain went into complete silence mode, and she didn't see or hear anything. She couldn't make out another word Paul said. Her brain seemed to just buzz with new understanding.

"Ruby? Hey, Ruby? Are you still there?"

"Did you just..." She swallowed thickly. The phone trembled against her ear. Her whole body shook. "Are you talking about one of the girls? Is that what you're saying?"

He had to be. If he wasn't, she didn't know what she would do. She might actually fire him if he got her hopes up like that, just to dash them later.

"Better than that. I've been speaking to three young ladies and their partners for the better part of three hours. This is them. They've been looking for you, too."

Three. He found three young women.

And they wanted to see her.

"Are you sure? You're sure it's them?"

Her voice sounded strained even to her own ears, but that was all right. She didn't care. Her heart was going to burst right out of her chest, and the sense of a gentle pressure on her shoulder was the thing that stopped her body from swaying.

She didn't look back. She wouldn't see anyone there, but it almost felt like Ryan was there with her. Just as eager as she was, laughing and telling her to take a breath and relax.

It would be just what he'd say when something massively overwhelming happened.

"They've given me their IDs to look at," Paul continued. "At this point, the only thing needed to confirm it would be a DNA test, but I've got the red panda you've already met, plus two lovely raccoon shifters who are eager to meet you. They're happy that you would like to see them, too."

"Of course I do! Where are you? I'll come to see you."

They had to be at one of the hotels in town.

Ruby was kicking herself for how she'd behaved in the bakery earlier. She'd thought that young woman was one of Angela's spies. Someone sent to make sure Ruby wasn't stepping out of line.

No, it was one of her nieces coming to feel out her welcome, and Ruby had been so... so cold and rude.

"Easy, we'll come to you. We can meet at a restaurant

or your place. There are six people in total with their mates."

Their *mates*. Happiness bloomed inside of Ruby like a shining, overdue flower. The girls were happily mated. Maybe even had babies of their own.

She told herself to slow down and not get ahead of herself. Paul didn't say anything about children.

For the moment, the three girls and their mates were *more than enough*.

"They can come here. I want them to see Ryan's house. I... I'll make some food for them. Did they eat? Do they need anything?"

She half expected Paul to laugh at her.

"You can do whatever you need to do to feel comfortable, but I think they only want to sit down with you and listen to your side of the story." He definitely sounded like he was smiling over the phone, but he kept it as professional as could be. "I didn't tell them much. I thought that should be for you."

His voice was lowered, and for the first time, Ruby wondered if he had any privacy while speaking to her on the phone.

"So... what do they know?"

"They don't know that the mother passed. I believe they suspect your brother is, however. They've been looking around town, and Roquette mentioned searching obituaries and stopping by the cemetery before they checked into their rooms."

Ruby's throat tightened. She was just an aunt. A

consolation prize. The girls undoubtedly were looking for their parents, just to learn both were gone.

Ruby didn't know exactly what they knew, but she would make sure one of those things they walked away with was that their father loved them and didn't want to give them up.

"Okay, all right. Please, tell them they're all more than welcome here. So, Ray and Roquette. Who's the third?"

"Rita."

All Rs. Ruby pressed her hand to her face, her throat closing. It was one of the traditions from Ruby's side of the family. She didn't know if that was a coincidence or maybe the only thing their mother had been able to give before Angela wrenched them away from her.

But at least they got that. Something from Ryan's side.

She would give them the rest. Anything she could.

"I want to see them. I definitely want to talk to them. How soon can you get here?"

She gave Paul her address, and he promised to be there in twenty minutes.

God, she was so damn happy she'd hired him.

CHAPTER
NINE

All Ruby could think about while she waited for Paul to get to her house with her nieces—she could still hardly believe he found them!—was how damn messy her place was.

The dishes had to be shoved into the dishwasher immediately, the countertops wiped, trash taken outside to the bins, and if there was a spare piece of clothing sitting anywhere it shouldn't be, she immediately grabbed it and threw it into the hamper in her room.

Ruby made sure to close the door to her room because that was a disaster that she wouldn't be able to clean up within the next five minutes.

She had no time to sweep up, mop the floor, wash the windows, or do any of the other things she would have liked to if she'd had prior notice of incoming visitors.

Just to make sure her house didn't smell like anything unpleasant, she lit a couple of cinnamon roll candles. The smells of her bakery always calmed her down, and when three vehicles pulled up to the side of her house, she was satisfied that the place didn't look half bad.

But all that left her mind when she stepped out onto the porch, her heart racing while Paul exited his truck with a soft smile on his face.

In that moment, Paul was her angel, but Ruby could only pay attention to the people leaving the two other cars.

From the back passenger door of the first car, the red panda woman—Ray—stepped out, the tall bear shifter man sliding out with her, taking her hand.

Ray's mate. She had a mate supporting her and protecting her, and Ruby was so happy that she could have such a thing.

Then, Ray and Ruby's eyes met.

Ruby's throat started to close. She took a slow, deep breath, forcing herself to be calm, to not lose her composure. She was the elder. The aunt. The one who had to be strong and allow these three young women to feel whatever they needed to at this moment.

The other two ladies joined Ray.

They looked... similar. Their features did, at least. Each had a different hair color. Ray's red, and then a brunette and a white-blond.

Paul had said the other two were raccoon shifters, like Ryan.

The similarities with her brother were there. Ruby thought they might even look a little like her.

She forced a smile and opened her mouth to cheerily

tell them to come on inside. She would fix them some coffee and tea!

But instead, her voice cracked, and all that came out was a sob, and Ruby broke down like a little girl, holding her hands over her mouth.

They were here. Finally, they were actually here!

She didn't need a DNA test. These were her brother's babies. Absolutely, positively, without a doubt, she was looking into the faces of her family. Into the faces of the last pieces of her brother left on this Earth.

The three women at the bottom of the porch looked at each other, figuring out what to do before Ray led them forward onto wooden porch steps.

They likely meant to ask her if she was all right, and one of them reached out, placing her hand on Ruby's shoulder.

But Ruby wasn't having any of that. Still sobbing, she reached out, her arms grabbing for all three of them, yanking them into a hug so she could hold them tightly.

It was the same hug she knew Ryan would want to give them if he were there.

They hesitated, but when their arms came around her, they squeezed her back just as tightly.

"I'm so... so *happy*," Ruby said, wishing she had better words, wishing she had some way of making them understand just how grateful she was, how she was never going to be the same after this.

Even if they went on with their lives after this and wanted nothing more to do with her ever again, it was so monumentally relieving to know *they were all right.*

They were here, and they were safe.

"I'm so happy."

RUBY EVENTUALLY GOT a grip and invited the girls and their very tall, very muscular, and very handsome mates into the house, along with Paul.

She only had tea, coffee, or soda to offer for refreshments, and not for the first time, Ruby desperately wished she was more prepared. She was always baking, always had something on the go, except the one damn time when it mattered the most.

The biscuits offered were from a box, but it would have to do.

The girls didn't seem to notice the general clutter of the house or mind the lack of choice in refreshments. Very quickly, even Ruby forgot about it as she sat down at the kitchen table to listen to their stories.

Rita and Roquette were a little closed off about their chosen career paths, which could mean a couple of different things coming from raccoon shifters, but Ruby was thrilled when Ray shyly admitted that she was a working artist.

"That's wonderful!"

Ray shrugged, though she smiled and blushed as her fingers played with her mug. "Nothing really special. Most of my designs end up on napkins and tissue boxes."

"Are you kidding me? That's still amazing! Can I get

those napkins for my store? Where can I buy them? A website?"

Ray appeared shocked from her spot across the table, but Rita and Roquette grinned, and Bill seemed the proudest of everyone while Ray explained the tissues and napkins were sold in big box stores.

Ruby promised Ray that she would go out and buy up as many packages as she could right away—after Ray sent her an image of what the designs looked like, of course. She didn't want to bulk-buy someone else's designs!

The group spoke a lot, especially about Ryan. Ruby hated that the story she had to tell the girls about their father was such a sad one. He lost his parents, his fated mate, and his daughters, and then he passed away far too young.

"But he never gave up hope," Ruby reassured them. "It was the bright spot for him. It was what kept him going each day. What kept the smile on his face. He was the kind of person who always looked forward to tomorrow and the promises that came with it."

Ruby wished she could tell them what happened to their mother and what her thoughts were on her daughters, but Ruby didn't have those answers for them.

Ruby had her own thoughts about the woman who let herself be bullied into giving up her own children by her bitch of a mother, but with Rita, Roquette, and Ray sitting at her table, Ruby held her tongue on that.

There were parts of the story Paul could confirm through his own hard work and digging, though he refused to accept any credit for the find. "You found each other. You all did the majority of the work."

Ruby wasn't quite sure she agreed with that.

It was thrilling, knowing her three nieces had also been seeking her out, the Baer sisters assisting them along the way, but she didn't want to give zero credit for the work Paul did either.

Their constant meetups and updates, his tedious work of going through every record he could get his hands on, and then dealing with all of Angela's bullshit...

Even if her nieces *had* also been looking, it didn't feel right to say that Paul had no hand in reuniting them.

"You came to the motel, though," Roquette said. "We might have stuck around in town, checking in with the bakery and the red pandas for days before we finally worked up the nerve to say hello."

Ruby brought her tea to her lips, taking a drink to hide the fresh wave of shame she felt for distrusting Ray as she did.

If Ray kept coming around with no explanation... Ruby shivered to think of what she might have said. Her anger over Angela's family and constant interference could have ended up getting the better of her.

In her worst nightmare, Ruby imagined herself confronting Ray, telling her to leave, and then, not knowing what she'd done, never seeing her ever again.

Yes. For that alone, Paul was worth every penny she owed him. And then some.

Ruby was still getting used to everyone being in her

house, of her nieces finally being real, and so far, what she knew of them, she liked.

"Do you girls need a place to stay? There's room here for you and your mates."

There really wasn't, but Ruby was determined to make it work. She had a couch that folded out, some extra blankets, and an air mattress. There were only two bedrooms in this house, so some people could be bunking up.

"It's all right," Rita said, her hand holding Dallas' tightly on the table. "We've all bought ourselves some rooms. I'm okay with heading back."

To Ruby's dismay, Roquette and Ray seemed to agree with this, each mentioning they did not wish to intrude.

Ruby made the offer again, insisting it would not be intruding at all, but again she was politely denied.

She decided not to press it. So long as the offer was out there, it would have to do. She reminded herself that her nieces didn't know her.

Not yet.

She wanted to get to know them, and since she was in the middle of her first impression, it was best to not let them think she was some crazy woman who would sulk if she didn't get her way.

In the end, they all agreed to go out to breakfast tomorrow.

Ruby could barely afford to keep her doors closed for the day, but Stephanie had an appointment that morning, and Ruby couldn't call her in.

"Paul?"

Paul straightened a little from where he'd been leaning against the wall, arms crossed, looking very much as though he was trying to blend in with the background.

"Yes?"

She hated doing this, especially in front of the girls and their mates. "I'm really sorry. I hate to ask you for another favor—"

He was already smiling at her. "Don't be sorry. Shoot."

"Your aunt and your dad made an order from the bakery for tomorrow. I will go in early and make sure it's done, but could you just ask them to call me before they arrive to pick it up?"

"Yes, I can do that. They won't mind." Paul nodded, giving her a warm smile that caused her stomach to flutter.

"Thanks."

It was her living, but it suddenly felt like a waste of time to be in the bakery when she could be learning more about the lives of her nieces.

Considering their mates all seemed to have a number of... implants—cybernetic enhancements that were either obvious or subtle—she wanted to know everything there was to know about them.

She didn't want to be doing any baking when there was so much to know.

"My dad is supposed to be laying off the sugar anyway," Paul said with a shrug.

"Really?" Ruby blinked. "Uh, I can cut out a quarter of

the sugar from the muffin recipe he ordered."

Paul's shoulders actually sagged. "Yes, please do that. I should've asked you earlier, to be honest."

"Paul, don't hesitate in any requests." She wanted to bake him all the cookies and all the cakes in the world, but it wouldn't be close to enough to make up for what he'd done for her.

Paul cleared his throat, pushing away from the wall. "Right, well, I'm going to take my leave."

"You're going?" Ruby was suddenly on her feet. She looked down at her nieces and their mates and then at Paul.

She didn't want him to go. She really didn't want him to leave. The idea of him walking out of her door made her feel like the family would be incomplete.

Because he's your mate, her inner raccoon said, not for the first time, but this time it was louder than ever before.

"This is for family, and you now have my reports, but give me a call if you need anything. Same goes for you all," he said, nodding down at Ray, Roquette, and Rita.

Though Paul's expression was a little cooler when he looked at Aaron. "See you around."

Aaron pursed his lips. "You, too."

Ruby glanced between both men as she sank back to her seat, and it wasn't lost on her the way Aaron's metal hand clenched and unclenched until well after Paul closed the front door behind him.

She heard his truck start and the engine hum before the sound trailed away, and he was gone.

"Uh, well, that was…" She had no idea what to say to that, but luckily she didn't have to.

"Don't mind him." Roquette laughed and slapped Aaron on his metal shoulder. "They just got into a fight before we came here."

"They *what*?"

Aaron growled under his breath, his shoulders hunching as if he was trying to vanish.

Good luck with a frame like that.

Ruby still couldn't believe it. "Sorry, say that again?"

In the hour she'd known them, she'd assumed that all of her nieces had married nice, boy-next-door types. She supposed she should have realized better after looking at their many implants. They clearly had been involved with… something. No one ended up with arms, eyes, and legs like that unless they were for a purpose.

To fight.

Roquette brought her tea back to her lips, hiding a blush. "It… might've been a little my fault."

"It wasn't your fault. It was his," Aaron growled, and his eyes actually turned red.

Even without that, Ruby could sniff out the angry testosterone of a protective male from a mile away.

"Paul came to our room and was looking around," Roquette continued. "And we thought he… might've been there on behalf of someone else."

"Do I want to know who you were keeping an eye out for?" Ruby asked.

"Probably best you don't know," Dallas said.

Ruby nodded, looking over her nieces. Whom she

only just got back into her life. "Are you all right? Is there anything I can do? Anything at all."

Not that there was much a baker in debt from a tiny, middle-American town could do, but if there was something, she was damn well going to figure it out.

"We're all right," Rita said. "Trust us, you don't have anything to worry about. The men can just be a little jumpy where we're concerned."

Typical good, protective mates, Ruby thought with a smile. She glanced at Dallas, whose shoulders bunched up and made him look like an offended hedgehog.

The two other men did too, after Rita's words, but Ruby had to admit, it brought her joy to see them all so happy with each other.

"Okay, but just so long as you all know, you've got a place to stay if you're ever in the area, or ever need any help." She had to stop herself before she could do something like offer gas money.

From the looks of the two cars outside, they earned more than she did, but she couldn't help herself. She still felt that urge to provide for her family however she could.

She liked to think part of it was Ryan, who wanted nothing more in his life than to have a chance to care for his girls. Maybe he was channeling that feeling down through her.

"Do you want to see photos of your father?" Ruby asked, getting up from the table.

The girls nodded and followed her to where the family photos were kept.

CHAPTER

TEN

They ended up staying another hour after Paul left.

Ruby wished it was longer. The second hour seemed to fly by as she showed them around the house their father had worked so hard for and then guided them through all the photos she had of him.

The photos of their birthday touched them the most.

"He thought about you every day of his life, but every year on your birthday, he made sure the rest of us did, too." Her cheeks reddened, and she suddenly felt bashful showing off the most recent photos, the last ones before he died. "It wasn't ever anything big. I'd bake a cake, or some cupcakes, put on some candles, and he'd blow them out for you. It was how he honored you."

Even though Ryan was smiling in the photo, she remembered every time they'd done it. It was never a particularly happy day.

Ryan seemed worried he would forget he had daughters, and looking back, Ruby thought he wanted some sort of connection. Anything at all, and that was why he wanted to blow out the candles.

Ruby worried that she would have to make more explanations, to go into details about how Ryan really wasn't happy smiling in those photos, but she didn't have to worry about defending his motives.

Her nieces appeared touched by the gesture, and Roquette wiped at misty eyes.

"I wish we could have met him," Ray said.

Ruby smiled down at her photo album. "I know he'd be proud of all of you. You turned into such beautiful, accomplished women. I think he would even approve of your mates."

They chuckled a little wetly at that, but Ruby's heart hurt as much as she was sure theirs did.

Ryan wasn't here to enjoy this. He wasn't here to threaten their mates with physical violence if they didn't treat his girls right, and he wasn't ever going to be here for their birthdays going forward.

Ruby would never forgive Angela for that.

At least she could do those things for Ryan, and she was sure that wherever Ryan was, he was glad his girls had been found and were safe.

When the couples left her house that night, Ruby waved from the door, watching as they drove off.

It took her a few minutes before she could get back into the house and clear away the mugs from their coffees.

And then she was too hyped up. Too excited. She felt like she'd just drowned herself in Redbulls.

Sleep was absolutely not coming to her that night. All Ruby wanted to do was wait for tomorrow, when she could see the girls again.

Because all she could do was toss and turn for a few hours, she was able to get to the bakery extra early.

She was usually there by five most mornings, so extra early meant *extra early*.

She got her orders done for the day, boxed them up, and put them into the car so she could deliver them to Paul's family when they were ready.

But after cleaning up, she was nice and early to the local diner known for excellent breakfast and brunch.

She grabbed a table and waited nervously for the girls to arrive.

What if they decided not to come? What if they didn't want to bother with her?

After all, they barely knew her, and she'd answered as many questions as she could about Ryan. If that was all they needed, she couldn't exactly stop them from leaving. Going on with the lives they'd had before they met Ruby.

She swallowed thickly, gripping the menu tight enough to put a dent in the plastic. Every time she heard the bell above the door chime, her head popped up.

She ducked back down quickly when it wasn't them and kept glancing at her phone.

Ruby breathed a relieved sigh when it finally buzzed.

A message from Rita.

They had slept in and were twenty minutes late but would be there in five.

Her heart finally stopped hammering.

When they arrived, Rita, Roquette, Ray, and their mates all offered apologies and showed sincere embarrassment. They asked if she had been waiting long and said how sorry they were, explaining that Rita had set Dallas' phone, but it didn't go off.

Ruby waved it all off, gratefully accepting their hugs, glowing as they all took their seats.

"Wasn't waiting long at all," she lied. "This stuff happens. I'm surprised you all managed to get up so early without an alarm."

"These guys are like a real alarm," Roquette said, grabbing Aaron's shoulder and giving it a soft shake. "Early birds, these ones."

Ruby could only smile, the anxiety of a few minutes ago entirely forgotten.

She still glanced up, however, searching. "Where… is Paul coming? I've got his order for his family."

She'd sent him the text and the invite to breakfast.

Maybe he slept in, too. The guy earned it with how hard he'd worked.

"I didn't see him," Aaron said, holding onto his menu and not at all sounding like he was sad Paul wouldn't be joining them.

Ruby sent another text Paul's way.

Even if Paul couldn't come, she wanted him to know she would drop off his father's order at his house after breakfast, but the invite was still open even if he turned out to be a little late.

When she put her phone away, Ruby paused.

Her nieces were all looking at her, knowing looks on their faces while the men put their entire focus on what they could order for breakfast.

"What?" Ruby felt a strange warmth rise up in her stomach, chest, and face. "What's the matter?"

"The coyote shifter," Roquette said, her lips curled at the side.

"Are you dating?" Ray asked eagerly.

"No!" Ruby replied immediately, feeling more heat hitting her and hitting hard. It embarrassed her more than she thought it would, though she couldn't figure out why.

"How long have you known each other?" Rita asked.

"Just these past few months. He's not from around here, but he comes into town to meet about the case."

"So you found your fated mate while trying to find us?" Roquette squealed. "That's so great!"

"Woah, who said fated mates?" Ruby objected.

"Your face," Ray answered.

"His face," Rita added with a roll of her eyes.

"No, it's nothing like that. He's kept everything strictly professional."

Sort of. Ruby supposed that getting his family involved to give her more business, taking smaller payments, and meeting up for all those coffees probably wasn't considered professional in the strictest of terms.

But that felt like a good kind of professionalism. Like he was just a really kind person who went above and beyond for his clients.

"Aren't you interested, though?" Roquette asked.

"He's a good-looking guy. You'd make a good pair."

"Watch who you call good-looking," Aaron gruffed, reaching for his water and giving his mate a side-eye.

Roquette leaned in nice and close, kissing him on the cheek and patting his arm as if she knew he was behaving like a child and didn't mind.

"Nothing is going on. I think I'm a little too old for starting up romances, anyway," Ruby said.

Even the men at the table were startled, as if she'd just said something outlandish.

"You're not too old," Ray said, aghast.

Ruby rolled her eyes, but this all felt good. They were actually having a meal, complete with family banter. It was amazing, and she'd forgotten the little annoyances that came with it.

She missed Ryan.

"Come on," Ray said, smiling at Ruby as if she didn't believe it for a second. "There is something there, we could see it plain as day. We saw it when he was asking us questions, as a matter of fact."

"Yeah," Roquette joined in. "Like, you would have thought he was our uncle, the way he quizzed us so hard and then looked so happy when he could finally conclude we were the family you were looking for."

"It was exactly how you'd expect a mate to behave on behalf of their other half." Rita shrugged matter-of-factly.

The waitress came over then with their food. The men impressed Ruby with the sheer magnitude of meat and eggs and pancakes they stuffed down their throats.

The ladies' meals were smaller and consisted of more fruit. Then it was teas, juices, and coffees.

Unlike the night before, their conversation centered less on their father and more on Ruby, which was a shock. She didn't think there was much to tell about herself. She'd worked and sacrificed so much of her free time to own her bakery and was currently living in her brother's house.

A house she assured the girls would belong to them if they only said the word.

Which they, in turn, assured her they never would.

The topic stayed off of the red panda family. Ruby felt a little badly for Ray about that. Maybe even a little badly for Angela. That woman didn't know what she was missing out on, and if she didn't regret it now, she might in the future.

"Are you okay with us coming to visit from time to time?" Ray asked at one point. "We would either come alone or together but would never be in your way."

Ruby blinked. Stunned. "You... *yes!* Absolutely. You'll always have a room to stay in at the house. If all of you come over and you don't want to pay for a room, I can make things work for all of you at the house."

She wished they felt close enough to her now to do just that, but Ruby had resigned herself that it would take more meals together. More time. Maybe even months or years before they felt comfortable enough to do that.

She could do it.

Ruby was sure of it, and not just for her brother's

sake.

She wanted to get to know her nieces. They were old enough that Ruby could start off as their friend first. They didn't grow up with her. They didn't know her as a protective adult or authority figure in their lives, but maybe someday they could look to her as someone who could offer advice... or whatever aunts did.

Slow and steady would win this race, but by their eager smiles, how her girls—*her girls!*—leaned into every conversation and seemed keen to ask after her love life, Ruby was confident she had a decent head start.

Like their meet-up the previous evening, breakfast came to an end way too damn fast.

The restaurant was even starting to slow down, and only a few stragglers were remaining before the lunch crowd started arriving.

The servers were starting to look at Ruby's table with annoyance, wanting them to pay and leave so they could clean up and prepare for the next group.

Ruby was sad when her girls pointed out they had some calls of their own to make, people to chat with.

The name Baer came up multiple times.

Right, the women who united her nieces. Ruby supposed it only made sense that they would want updates as well.

Ruby tried to grab the whole bill for herself, but Dallas followed her to the cashier and forced his card onto the young lady standing behind the counter.

"Don't take any of her money. I'm paying."

"I can pay for your meals," Ruby said, even though

that was barely true. With seven people at a table, the bill was nearly two hundred dollars after taxes—and that was before the tip.

"I got it," Dallas said, taking the terminal and typing in his password. "It means a lot to Rita and the others that you've been so kind and accepting toward them. Let me do this."

She wasn't entirely sure if he was just saying that to make her feel better or if it was a little true.

Maybe a little of both.

But Ruby was the oldest, and she couldn't allow herself to stand by and do nothing while the mate of one of her nieces paid for the whole table.

"Okay, then I'll at least get the tip, she said, fishing out the last of her bills and grateful she'd bothered with keeping them.

She gave forty dollars to the woman behind the counter for their tip pot, knowing it wasn't as much as they probably would have liked for such a big table, but she only had the two twenties on her.

The young lady smiled softly anyway and accepted the money with thanks.

On the way out, while grabbing her purse and heading for the door with the girls, Ruby was pretty sure she saw Bill set another couple of bills down on the table anyway.

She sighed and decided to leave it be. Part of having a family was how they all took care of each other, and she needed to get used to that again.

It was a good problem to have.

CHAPTER

ELEVEN

"You know, you should ask out Paul."

Ruby tensed up, shocked that Ray would suggest such a thing as they exited the diner.

"I don't think he's interested."

Roquette and Rita were checking messages with their mates, and Ray took the brief distraction to pull Ruby aside, signaling to Bill that she would only be a minute.

"I do think he's interested in you. *Very* interested. We all do."

Ruby didn't think she'd ever blushed so much in her entire life. Her whole body felt so hot that she might as well turn into a red panda herself.

Ray just kept looking at her with that knowing little smirk and a slight shake of her head. "He definitely had eyes that were only for you last night. You didn't notice?"

"I... I'm sure he was just worried. I'm his client."

"Right," Ray said, still smiling, still glowing. "Because I'm sure that part of being a PI includes personal introductions and then hanging around for an hour to make sure things all turned out swell. Isn't his job just to dig for info and report it to you?"

Could it be true? Ruby had tried so hard to talk herself out of believing it, but with Ray saying it, she started to wonder.

"You think so?" She finally asked.

"I do," Ray confirmed. "But it shouldn't be a question. If you have a fated mate sense toward him, then he *totally* will have it for you, too."

At Ruby's confused look, Ray continued. "Sometimes the fated mate sense isn't as clear as others make it out to be. Sometimes it's hard to trust our natural instincts, and it can just be confusing."

"Especially when you're my age."

Ray squinted her eyes in confusion. "Really? I thought we're supposed to get older and wiser with age, and more in touch with our intuition."

"In many ways, that's true." Ruby nodded. "But love? I've never mastered that one. I think believing in love and mates is easier when you're younger and less jaded."

"You don't seem jaded," Ray stated. "Even after losing your parents and brother. You told us yesterday that our father never gave up hope but look at *you*. You never gave up hope either."

"For finding you girls, yes," Ruby said.

"Finding us *was* finding love. Love of family. You believed in love. We could have ended up being total bitches, but that didn't matter to you. You took the risk, you didn't give up, and you should extend that determination to accepting the feelings toward your fated mate."

"You're really stuck on this fated mate thing, huh?" Ruby asked, though she knew good and well that the words had crossed her mind more than once since meeting Paul.

"Look, I'm no Esme Baer, but I just have a feeling about this. You don't have to take my word for it, though. Rita agrees too, and she's by far the most cynical of all of us. If she thinks so, that makes me even more certain."

Ray's words made her heart swell with the very hope she was encouraging. Paul... sexy, sweet, caring Paul could be her fated mate?

"It was definitely obvious he was into you." Ray stuffed her hands into her pockets, still smiling, though she shrugged as if trying to be casual. "I don't know, maybe now that you're not his client anymore, since we all came together and everything, you could maybe ask him out?"

"Me?"

"Why not?"

"I don't know," Ruby said.

Ryan always told her that her problem was that she was too shy when it came to men, and now, here was one of his daughters telling her that she needed to take a chance.

"Trust me," Ray said, pressing a hand to Ruby's shoulder, her eyes bright. "You should ask him first. He might be too shy or too caught up in being *professional* or whatever to make the first move."

Ruby looked at Ray hard. "You say that like you've got some insider knowledge on it."

Ray pulled her hand back, clearing her throat. "Right, well anyway, I'd like to come back and visit you in a few months and see you've got a" —she stopped herself, glancing back to Bill, making sure he couldn't hear her— "a hot man on your arm, like the three of us. Then it would come full circle, you know?"

Ruby wanted to laugh. She couldn't believe she was having this conversation.

But it was all right.

Now that she'd had it, she was feeling a little... braver.

"No promises," she said.

"That means a small promise," Ray said quickly, then she pulled Ruby into a quick hug and kissed her cheek. "Go for it."

Ruby nodded.

She said her last goodbyes to Rita and Roquette. There were more hugs and kisses. More promises to check in.

Ruby had all of their email addresses and phone numbers, and they'd all added each other on the various social media platforms.

She could actually send them messages and more photos.

Dallas, Aaron, and Bill shook her hand, and she made them promise not to be strangers.

They were going to be in the area for a bit. Apparently, there was some work that needed to be done, but they'd be around in the next couple of days before fully returning to their lives.

As they drove away, Ray felt a bittersweet sadness inside her.

She might see them a couple of times a year, but she at least had contact with them now. She could message them whenever she wanted.

She could get to know their children if they eventually had them.

She again wished that this could have happened when Ryan was around.

It was so weird, being so happy and so sad at the same time.

When she pulled herself into her car, forcing her eyes not to burn or her throat to close, her phone immediately pinged.

A group chat from Rita already:

Ray told us what she said. Definitely ask him out.

Ruby laughed.

Another message came in the same chat, this one from Roquette:

And give us all the details!

Ruby glanced into her back seat, where the boxes of carrot muffins and cakes were sitting for Roger and Cheryl, making her car smell pleasantly of cinnamon and spice.

She started her car.

Maybe she would ask him out. Right now, while she was still riding high on this good feeling.

CHERYL HAD TEXTED Ruby her address when Ruby contacted her to confirm that Paul had told her about the bakery's closing that day.

Cheryl had been understanding, even offering to come and get them the next day, but Ruby insisted she could drop them off, so now she had the address of the Lapin family.

She had to double-check her Google maps when she pulled up to make sure she had the right house. It was beautiful. Turn of the century, with a wrap-around deck and a couple of spires.

The paint was bright and looked new-ish, and the yard was green and lush with healthy grass, shrubs, and flower patches.

Numerous children shrieked as they chased each other around in the yard, but they immediately stopped when they spotted Ruby parking her car. They became much more interested when she pulled the boxes out.

Of course they did. Kids—especially shifter children —could smell sweets and sugar from across the continent.

They raced to her, and Ruby was left with the inter-esting task of trying not to drop the boxes as she waded through a hoard of eager kids, all asking questions about what she was carrying.

She made her way up the porch steps and to the door, where some of the kids gave up on her. One helpfully opened the door, and the rest of them rushed inside, leaving Ruby standing just outside.

"Hey, Grandma! There's a lady here with something for you!"

Ruby nearly laughed. She loved kids and how brazen they were.

Instead of Cheryl, or anyone else answering the calls of the excited kids, it was Paul who appeared around the corner.

Ruby froze.

His eyes widened at the sight of her, but he approached quickly. "Hey, I didn't realize you were coming over," he said, immediately taking the boxes from her.

"Uh, your, uh, aunt gave me the address for the drop-off."

"She did?" Paul asked. "She must have forgotten to tell me. She's in the attic shuffling through some old stuff."

They were silent for a minute.

Did Ruby look put together? She should have checked her lipstick before getting out of the car. She doubted any had lasted through breakfast.

She'd been up so long that she probably looked rough. Meanwhile, Paul was standing there all handsome and glowing in the morning light.

"Do you want to come in?" he offered.

"No, sorry. I didn't... I'll go. I just wanted to make sure you got these."

"No, please, come inside for coffee," Paul stepped out of the way for her. "I know you were up early."

"Yeah, pretty early." No way was she telling him that she hadn't slept a wink.

She stepped inside the house. The sounds of laughter were everywhere. It was bright. There were big windows everywhere, and the kitchen he brought her to was even brighter.

She was proud of the small house Ryan had bought and left for her, but this place made her home look like a run-down cottage in comparison. What did Paul think of it when she had him over last night?

"You live here?"

"No, moved out years ago," he said. "But we all get together for breakfast at least once a week. There are still sausages and some scrambled eggs. Would you like some to go with your coffee?"

He set the boxes down on what looked to be real marble countertops, and she saw the large food warmers set up.

"No thanks, I just came from breakfast. The men that Rita, Roquette, and Ray snagged for themselves can really eat." Then Ruby thought of something. "I'm so sorry. I didn't realize you were trying to have family time when I was texting you."

"It's fine, don't worry about it. Did you have a good time?"

He leaned against the counter, his arms loosely crossed, but he appeared as relaxed as could be, like he was genuinely curious.

Ruby felt a flush of pleasure at that.

Paul had been with her on this for months. She might have been paying him for it, but she also felt like she was at least talking to a friend. More than a friend. Someone who was almost as invested in the outcome of the case as she was.

"Very good. They've got some stuff to take care of, but they'll be in the area for the next few days. You might get some calls, but otherwise, we'll stay in touch."

Paul nodded. "That's good. That's what you were hoping for, right?"

"Yes, it was." Ruby rubbed the back of her neck. "I mean, it's amazing, considering how things could have been. They're together. They get to be sisters. I knew the chances of them living near me weren't so great, but we'll still get to see each other, and I'm on their Facebook."

The handsome crinkles that came around Paul's eyes whenever he smiled returned. "I'm glad."

He looked it, too.

He looked proud. Did he feel like that for all of his clients? Did he look like this for all of his clients? Ray didn't seem to think so. Roquette and Rita, either.

The flutter in Ruby's stomach amplified, and this time, instead of pushing it down, she let it swell.

Fated mate? She asked herself, and her raccoon replied immediately with a whoop: *yes!*

Time to shoot her shot. Ray seemed to think he would be too shy. He'd be concerned with keeping things professional, of not crossing the line with his client, despite the fated mate draw.

So Ruby had to be the one to do it.

"Yeah, I'm fine," she took a breath. "You want to grab a coffee sometime?"

He blinked at her. "Sure, but you don't have to worry about payments for another couple of weeks. Did you need an extension?"

Now it was her turn to blink, and then she chuckled softly. "No, I think with your family coming around the bakery as often as they do, I'll be able to afford to pay it all soon enough."

"They love carrot cakes."

"Yeah, so I've seen." Ruby nodded. "But I hope that we don't have to wait until I've paid up before we can go on a date."

There. She said it. She actually did it, and now if he said no, she would know for sure and be able to turn her attention somewhere else.

She was a big girl who made her own decisions, and she'd ripped off the Band-Aid.

Paul seemed shocked. He seemed frozen.

Ruby deflated a little.

"Yes," he said quickly. "Yes, I'd love to take you out."

"You would?"

"You sure that's all right with you? I don't want you to think you have to because of our working relationship."

Oh yeah, definitely on the far spectrum of professionals.

But that was okay. She liked that about him. She thought it was endearing.

"To be honest, Paul, it was because of our working relationship that I didn't allow myself to accept what my heart has been telling me since the moment I met you."

He moved closer to her, and this time, when he took her hand, he didn't let go. "Ruby, if you tell me that you feel we're fated mates, then my heart will soar because I've been trying not to think about it every moment of every day. You make me crazy, Ruby, from the food you make to every smile you give, I just can't get enough of you, and I've had to stop myself from making a move. I know it's not right, not until we get the work stuff settled."

She smiled, and despite herself, tears welled up in her eyes. "Well, how about we take things a little slow then? We go out, coffee, movies, dinner dates, but if you're worried about how it would look, we don't have sex until after I finish paying you in full."

The little muscle beneath Paul's eye twitched, and he actually looked slightly panicked before he huffed a breath and gave her a crooked, flirty smile. "I need to get my dad and Cheryl to make a lot more trips to your bakery."

Ruby laughed out loud at that. "Really?"

"You're my fated mate," Paul admitted. "And I've had to stop myself from making a move. From pushing you. God knows the last thing I wanted was to scare you off, but I really don't want to wait a year before I can touch you."

Her stomach fluttered, and more of that bravery filled her up from the inside out.

Ruby quickly glanced around, making sure no kids were spying.

She stepped closer to Paul, pressing her chest against his and reaching up to finally let her fingers run through his soft coyote-colored hair. His deep brown eyes seemed to dance as she gazed up into them.

"You can do a little touching," she said.

He was taller than she was. Over a head taller. She had to tilt her head high as she looked up at him.

And she had to go up on tiptoes so she could kiss him on the mouth.

The happy thrill she got for making the first move was nothing compared to the pleasure that came when his big hands rested on the small of her back and her waist and kissed her back.

This has been the best week of my life.

The End.

...almost!

Rita, Roquette, and Ray have finally reunited and found their family! But the vampire, Lilly, is still out there, furious at those who've stolen her soldiers from her. It won't be long before she makes her next move, in Etched in Brass (Shape Up or Shift Out Book 5)!

SHAPE UP OR SHIFT OUT SERIES

A Rose by Any Other Name
Winter of Discontent
Sea of Trouble
The Better Part of Valor
Etched in Brass

About the Author

USA Today Bestselling Author Mandy Rosko is a videogame playing, book loving chick. She loves writing paranormal romances that range from light steamy to erotic, and has some contemporary and historical romances as well. You can find her on all sorts of platforms, including Twitch, where she does writing sprints, crafting, and video gaming!

Get all the latest news from Mandy by signing up for her newsletter: subscribepage.com/mandyroskobooks

As a bonus for signing up, you'll get her starter library,

including Burns Like Fire, Sold to the Enemy, and The Vampire's Curse!

facebook.com/MandyRoskoRomance

instagram.com/mandyroskodraws

amazon.com/Mandy-Rosko/e/B008ETBVFW

bookbub.com/authors/mandy-rosko

goodreads.com/mandyrosko

youtube.com/UCD1z6r06dKoN-0WdUbi1pAQ

ALSO BY MANDY ROSKO

PARANORMAL ROMANCE

Blood Secrets

Darkness Awakened

Passion Awakened

Beauty Awakened (Coming Soon)

Eve Langlais' FUCN'A

I'll Be Dammed

Trash Queen

Chillin' Out

Bits and Bobs

Poisoned Kisses

Goddesses of Vengeance

Angel's Fury

Shape Up or Shift Out

A Rose by Any Other Name

Winter of Discontent

Sea of Trouble

The Better Part of Valor

Etched in Brass (Coming Soon)

Shifter Hospital

Alpha Medicine

Second Chance Alpha (Coming Soon)

The Aquaterrestrial Task Force

Get Kraken

Shark Bait

The Nightshade Guild

Mage to Disobey

Magic Confined

Defying Time

Crimson Moon Hideaway

(Amazon and KU Only)

Double Booked with Her Ex

Flame and Mist

Learn more at mandyrosko.com